Echo Three Tango

Echo Three Tango

By
Dennis K. Hausker

Strategic Book Publishing and Rights Co.

Strategic Book Publishing & Rights Co., LLC
USA | Singapore
www.sbpra.com

For information about special discounts for bulk purchases, please contact Strategic Book Publishing and Rights Co. Special Sales, at bookorder@sbpra.net.

ISBN: 978-1-948858-13-7

Chapter One

Staff Sgt. Brady Black took off his helmet for a moment to mop his brow, but only because sweat was rolling down his forehead into his eyes on this humid and stressful day. He couldn't afford to be distracted for even a second. Here, in this moment, that could mean swift death. Battles were always terrifying, but in this case, more so than ever before in his personal history in the corps. Although Brady was accustomed to having jangled nerves in a fight, this time his instinctive fear responses from so many near misses affected him greatly. That was very much out of character for a superb soldier who prided himself on controlling his emotions under any circumstances, battle or otherwise.

The scene on this planet, called Grailon, gave him an overwhelming impression of green as the foliage ran rampant with plush, nearly continuous, forests choked with thick undergrowth. That, combined with high humidity in the atmosphere, made for an uncomfortable existence, made worse by the strenuous fighting, all while running for his life. Additionally, strong, pungent scents flooded his perceptions, which was another departure from the usual norm in their fights. However, he didn't have time to stop and ponder whether those scents were dangerous, toxic-like poisons. War had come to this particular "Garden of Eden," and he was mired in the middle of it.

Brady was gasping from the rigors of battle, and his heart was thumping. These forays into the unknown were never easy against enemy combatants as diverse as the mind could imagine. What tended to be true nearly every time was that they were engaging devoted opponents who were backed into near-suicidal situations, often defending family and friends at all cost. Abject rage seemed to be a common emotion in all species on all planets, and that made them supreme threats.

His unit, Echo Three Tango, or E3T, had a reputation for superior skills, tenacity, and "finding a way" no matter the challenge or the opponent that they'd earned over a long period of time.

However, this time, not only were the enemy fighters stubborn beyond belief, they were succeeding, and that was very distressing. They were huge, fierce, resourceful, adaptive, savage creatures who were willing to die to the last fighter if need be, sacrificing themselves to extravagant extent to bleed their enemy. It was a meat grinder of a battle and was nowhere near to being finished. Being the perennial "invader" was never a role Brady was comfortable with, but like it or not, that was the job in the corps; they followed orders.

Overhead, air battles were as hotly contested as the ground actions, though the corps pilots were having better success than the ground forces. It was a strange scene for Brady to look up at the popping sounds like he was watching holiday fireworks displays, but those were real battles and living beings who were dying on both sides up there.

He tensed at movement to his right, shifting his aim to face any emerging threat. Jocol Kukuk rolled out of the undergrowth, bumping against Brady. He was a massive being, one of many nonhuman members of E3T, and he was wounded.

"Jocol, hold still, you're hit." Brady quickly opened his first aid field kit to press a thick bandage against a serious, seeping wound in Jocol's leg. Taping it rapidly, they both scanned all around the area for a brief moment, searching for imminent threats, while they considered what to do next.

Jocol moaned and grimaced. However, he still remained vigilant for any new enemy attacks, in spite of the injury. Seeing Jocol look worried was a first for Brady.

"Can you walk?"

"I don't know."

After taping the bandage, hoping it would staunch the flow of life fluids long enough to get medical aid, Brady helped Jocol to his feet.

Jocol muttered, "I was stupid. It was right there hiding, but I didn't use proper caution going into that thicket. I got it, but it shot me first."

"This is their world. They know it like we don't, and they're fighting for their lives, and probably their families' lives too."

"I know that," Jocol snapped. He was annoyed with himself, and it came out in his tone.

"Maybe we should ease back to the camp to get you treatment?"

"No, I'm not going to back down because of my own stupidity."

"Macho isn't smart in combat. In the corps, we prevail in these wars because we don't make those kinds of ego mistakes. That's a serious wound you can't just ignore."

An air fight came to an end just above them, with the losing enemy craft crashing very near to Brady and Jocol. It forced them to rush, backing out of the way of the impact. At that point, Brady dragged Jocol along and kept them going away from the front, heading toward the rear to their forward fire base.

Jocol grumbled, but he didn't resist. He was in pain because of his serious wound, and he had great difficulty trying to limp along. Jocol was a very large and heavy being, and Brady propped him up as best he could as they staggered along, but it was slow going.

The farther they went toward the rear, the more comrades they saw retreating in similar distress; they were wounded and in need of medical treatment. The trickle of movements around them turned into a significant flow of injured troops, far more than Brady ever remembered seeing in any prior fight, and he'd seen many.

Behind them, they could hear the strange sounds the enemy troops made in battle: vocalized, unison grunts, roars, clicks, and various ululations; none of it was coherent speech. It was intended to terrorize, and it did. Even for superb, hardened combat veterans like E3T, it was daunting to hear. For the first time, Brady wondered if there could be a victorious outcome here. Adding to his terror were memories of seeing what had happened when the enemy had trapped E3T soldiers. They faced savage death by being literally torn apart in front of their comrades. These enemies were huge and powerful adversaries, physical specimens that matched any troops Brady had ever seen. *Mano-e-mano* fights in close quarters were the last possible options to consider, as that outcome usually was not good.

The camp was in turmoil, with too many wounded soldiers flooding in to handle. It meant the situation at the front lines was desperate.

To make matters even worse, E3T was diverse both in having numerous different species, and also with having some females from those species included in the frontline combat troops. This particular enemy showed no mercy whether they encountered male or female troops. Females were subjected to equal horror at the hands of this savage and bloodthirsty horde.

However, Brady noticed in the midst of the mayhem, these enemy troops weren't undisciplined berserkers racing about out of control. They had a plan—and locating officers to eliminate those controlling the allies' battle movements was high on their list of goals. Having E3T officers suddenly butchered and eliminated left the troops without direction and forced them to make individual command decisions, which was not a good development in the middle of a serious fight. Coordinating combat operations was critical to winning any battle.

The sounds of fighting grew closer as the frontline defeats were compounded from a sustained setback toward an outright rout. A medic rushed up to examine Jocol's wound. They quickly jammed an injection of Formula Twenty-three, the miraculous and instant regenerating fluid, into the injured area, which brought rapid healing and quickly left the injured area repaired and like new. The compound was a remarkable discovery, as it adapted to use the genetic code of any species to instantly replicate healthy tissue to repair wounds.

Within moments, Jocol stood and flexed his leg. "I'm fine now. Let's go, Brady."

"Don't bother." Turning, they saw Captain Suzie Morgan jogging toward them. "We're in full retreat across the entire front. The plan is to try to regroup back here, but I question if that's even doable. The enemy is not breaking off the attack. They smell blood and are trying to end this war before it can get off the ground. I never thought I'd see this day, the corps in full retreat, running with our tails between our legs."

Suzie was the only officer Brady could see, other than the doctors, in this camp.

"What can we do, Suzie?"

"Well, Brady, we try to survive. I think the fleet will try to do an extraction, but with the enemy fighters mixed in among our units, I suspect that's not yet a viable option. So, we gather as many of our people as we can to become a functioning combat unit again. With these large-scale casualties, there are no units fully intact after that fiasco."

"How could this happen?" asked Jocol. "We're invincible. We never lose wars."

"Well, obviously these guys didn't get that memo. They are a scary bunch. Fan out and watch our troops coming into this camp. Direct any soldiers still in shape to fight over to the west, where we'll try to reorganize before the enemy attack gets here."

The three split up and hurried away in different directions.

Suddenly, the ground under Brady's feet shook from a distant, massive explosion.

"Wow, the fleet is opening up with planet busters. This isn't good," he muttered as he waded into the approaching troops.

Grabbing three nearby troops racing into the camp, they eyed him fearfully.

"Hey, get it together. Rok, Dorn, and Misty, we need you to focus. We're still the corps."

The three paused a moment to let Brady's words sink into their terrified brains. All three were from different races. Misty was a human woman, and a pretty one. She wasn't a person Brady would normally have thought to find in this elite combat unit.

"Are you okay, Misty?"

"Yeah, I . . .eh . . ."

"I know it was eye-opening seeing us get chewed up like that. How could the powers that be miss this level of danger without proper preparations? Who's making these decisions?"

"I don't know, but I'd like a couple of minutes alone in a room with them. We lost a lot of good people today, friends from . . . well . . . forever."

"Head over to the west. Suzie Morgan is trying to set up a staging area to get us back in the fight."

"Duh, what fight?"

"It beats sitting here waiting to be slaughtered. Grab anybody else you see as you go."

"Sure thing, Brady."

"Move them along, as we have no time to waste."

Brady grabbed more of his comrades, both troops that carried wounded comrades, and those wounded troops recently healed, like Jocol had been. He could see the quickly growing mass of E3T soldiers clustered around Suzie, listening to her as she barked out instructions. No other officers had made it back, so far.

Another massive explosion shook the ground, this time closer than the last.

An air battle started directly overhead, but this time the allies' low-altitude, fast-attack, fighter craft wings were joined by heavy cruisers that descended from their normal deployment of protecting the fleet in space. That meant much heavier weapons had just joined the fight, and it showed up quickly in favorably tipping the air battles. The allied craft changed their battle tactics to allow clear shots for the cruisers, although that was fraught with danger for the ground troops, as those salvos kept going and hit the ground. Getting out of the way was virtually impossible. Survival at that point was more a matter of luck than skill.

The air battle finally seemed winnable, as the enemy craft had no vessels able to contend with the cruisers. This did nothing for the ground forces, however. The best that could occur was to make windows for sporadic evacuations up to the fleet.

The allied army continued to retreat, condensing into tighter rings of concentrated troops. Heavy thumps of continuing bombardment from space seemed to dampen the enemies' fervor slightly, which gave the E3T soldiers some time to separate and regroup.

Brady looked up to see the start of continuous transport flights traveling up to space. Suzie looked up too. The transfer of surrounded ground troops up to the safety of the fleet in space was rapid, as they could move large numbers at a time. The large transport vessels were protected from the rapidly dwindling numbers of enemy light-surface fighter craft by waves of allied fighter craft patrolling all about. Once the air war turned against them, the enemy aircraft took a pounding.

"Okay, folks, it looks like somebody up there woke up finally and realized we needed to be out of here," Suzie said. "Our new mission is to protect the retreat. I strongly suspect this enemy isn't interested in simply watching us leave. They will exact a toll down to the last possible instant. Obviously, the last of us here will be in near suicidal situations. I'm making that task volunteer only."

The planet-buster, carpet-bombing tactics increased in frequency.

"Damn them," Jocol muttered.

"Are you talking about the enemy or our leadership?"

"Both. I didn't join this unit to die for no good reason. Why are we even here?"

"That's way above my pay grade. I have no idea."

"Brady, don't you feel we need to question what we do? I'm no coward about war, but honestly, I often feel I should be fighting with our enemies defending them against our own aggression, except now. These bastards are evil."

"I know, Jocol. I'm not immune from feeling guilty about some things. I do wonder what goes on in headquarters. Where do the orders originate? Who's telling the generals and admirals what to do?"

"Like Misty said, give me a few minutes alone in a room with them."

Brady smiled. "I'm okay with that."

They snickered, but it was a short respite. The steady flow of retreating troops transformed into a flood of soldiers of the corps, nearly all of them wounded to some extent.

Suzie's growing impromptu force quickly deployed to surround the camp. Fresh from a quick bite to eat and replenishing their ammo, they opened up with a withering, overlapping firing pattern into the enemy troops as they emerged into the clearing. Retreating troops joined them to present a large, solid, shoulder-to-shoulder circle of troops and weapons fire. Additionally, they created multiple tiers, the first rank lying on their bellies to fire, the next rank kneeling, and the next rank standing. It was the first success they had had against this enemy. Here also, they had the help of automated, mechanized, heavy-weapon gun emplacements with laser-controlled aiming devices. The concentrated firepower was far more than the surging, teeming enemy could overcome, and they incurred more casualties in moments than at any other time in the sustained battle. Their swarming tactics hurt them here where the allies could separate to get clear shots from the ground and from above.

Meanwhile, overhead, the air battle continued to be favorable enough that the steady succession of flights continued rapidly, moving large numbers of combat troops and support personnel out of harm's way up to the fleet in space. This enemy had shown no force able to attack the space fleet, and the fact they did nothing now indicated they had none. Their air operations had been restricted to planet-based fights, and those air operations were decreasing rapidly as corps air wings blasted them out of the sky.

At that point, the surrounding enemy horde seemed content to bide their time. With each passing allied flight up to space, their job got easier, as fewer allied weapons remained to dole out death.

Seemingly, their few remaining air vessels retreated into hiding, as they were being rapidly annihilated by superior allied aircraft controlled by superb pilots. Once the fearsome enemy ground troops stopped firing and merely sat in silence watching the defenders, it was eerie and frightening for the dwindling number of survivors.

The last-ditch volunteers included Brady.

"Listen, Suzie, I'm single. Let those married folks head out. They've got families waiting for them back home."

"Brady, that's very brave of you, but think about this. You've got an equal right to survive as married people do. Those killers won't wait long before they hit us, and getting out then will be . . . well, you know."

"If this is my time, so be it."

She shook her head. "I don't know whether to slug you or kiss you."

"I'll pick the kissing option."

They both chuckled, even under these fatal circumstances.

"Brady, you're an inspiration to me."

"Hardly. I'm just another infantry slug."

The reserve troops just behind the troops on the line were called back to depart. Now their jeopardy went up exponentially.

"Go, Captain. Say something nice about me at my funeral."

She kissed his cheek and then hustled to the waiting transport. By now, the nearby thumps of planet-buster weapons shook the ground so hard that anybody standing was knocked to the ground. That included the deployment of enemy soldiers too. It helped delay their final assault.

Even while lying on the ground, they started their verbal battle cries. This close, it was debilitating to hear, but the E3T rear guard had no intention of going out with a whimper. They started their own chant, that of the corps. It bolstered their courage, screaming in the face of certain death.

The enemy began to gesture and slowly rise up, standing and turning to face the survivors, like they were gathering their courage. However, the bombing hadn't ceased, and they were still being knocked off their feet. It was a daunting sight.

Brady glanced around. The narrow window for allied escape craft no longer existed. Between enemy ground fire, resumed attacks from their few remaining aircraft, and a shrunken knot of allied troops, there could no longer be suppressing fire from the fleet because it would hit them, the last guard.

"It would probably be better if the fleet took us out rather than leave us to the mercy of those monsters. Maybe we should agree to off each other rather than be captured," said Misty, another volunteer.

"I've never been somebody to give up," Brady replied. "We can't win this fight, so let's go with Plan B."

"What's Plan B?" asked Jocol.

"Sleight of hand."

"Huh?"

"We've got what, about a hundred of us left? We break up into small units, maybe five apiece. At my signal, as they attack, we use concussion grenades at them in total dispersal, but also the smoke and the concealing charges. We keep the automated, heavy gun emplacements firing continuously in every direction but south, then we slip away and fan out to live off the land."

Misty laughed. "You are seriously demented, my friend. Live off the land?"

"I prefer it to being prisoners to them. We've all seen what they do. Our lives as their entrée would be very short at that point."

Misty looked at Jocol, who shrugged. "Okay, you're on, Brady."

"Pass the word and get ready. We'll need to move fast toward the south before we split up."

"I'm going with you, Brady. Who else do you want?"

"I don't care, maybe Jocol, Sara, and Bontag. We're all right here together."

"Okay, you've got it."

"We've still got our comm units to stay in touch. Maybe the fleet will come up with a solution later."

"Don't hold your breath on that one. We're expendable. You do realize once we use up our ammo, there's no way to resupply and reload. We're helpless at that point."

"I'll come up with an answer . . . later."

"Right, Brady."

The enemy began to move, so Brady's plan went into play; they laced them with grenades, and also unleashed the smoke and the concealing charges. The survivors quickly arose *en masse* and raced southward. The enemy was confident of an easy victory at that point and didn't properly surround the survivors, so there were too few troops to the south. With the element of surprise with Brady's ploy, as unlikely as such a maneuver would work, it did. Leaving enemy soldiers dead in their wake, they sprinted away before Brady lifted his fist. At his signal, the prearranged groups of five each raced away in nearly every direction.

"Stay alive." It was his last order before they dispersed. "Find places you can hide. We talk every week to assess things and make an ongoing plan. Adjust to prevailing conditions, whatever you run into."

Brady sprinted at a dead run to get out of the clearing and into the cover of the nearby forest. Once they broke the tree line, they slowed to a steady but brisk jogging pace to put distance between them and the enemy soldiers.

"Bontag, take point, and be careful for enemy traps. They are diabolical. Jocol, guard the rear. Sara, Misty, watch each side. Let's make best time for as long as we can hold up."

Nobody spoke; they were busy breathing at the aggressive jogging pace. Slowing down was not an option.

Hurrying at the best pace they could sustain, hours passed as they covered ground. It seemed like a miracle the enemy wasn't in hot pursuit. The ground battle was over, but the bombardment was not, as they still felt massive thumps shake the ground.

"I guess the fleet isn't willing to forgive our loss. They're blasting the hell out of those bastards," Brady muttered.

"That works for me," Jocol replied.

"Let's rest for a few minutes. We're exhausted."

Moving up a small hill, they stopped, crouching in concealing underbrush.

"Just take a few swallows of water and limit it to one food packet. We need to stretch our supplies until we can figure out what to eat off this land and can find safe water sources."

"You really think we can stay alive, Brady?" Sara eyed him with uncertainty.

"I do. We've trained and fought all of our lives, preparing for survivor scenarios. This is just another test that we will pass."

"Right," said Misty. "We're all big people, Brady. You don't need to treat us like gullible infants."

"I'm not. We're going to find a way."

"You better. I'm not afraid to die, but how they would do it, it makes me shudder. Those bastards are vile. I can't get those images out of my mind. I actually saw them consume the bodies of our fallen, many of whom weren't dead."

"We all saw it, Misty. Let's not talk about it. We're going to make sure it doesn't happen to any of our survivors."

"They've got those huge mandibles where they can eat bodies whole. They're like a cross between reptilian and insect genetic roots. How is that possible?"

"I know. It's sickening. We'll be okay, though."

He looked around the group and saw the same skeptical expressions. Under the circumstances, he was also skeptical, but he didn't want to show it.

They tensed at a nearby sound. Two large animals ambled along a trail down below the hill where the unit had paused.

"Why don't we follow them to see where they lead us?"

"Great plan, Brady. They'll lead us right into the mouths of predators."

"They just might lead us to water, Sara."

They eyed each other.

"Do you have a better plan?"

Sara shrugged, shaking her head.

"Okay then, let's go."

The unit scurried back down the hill and followed the animals, but at a safe distance.

Both scenarios came true. An hour later, the animals had led them to water, and they were attacked by predators, a pack of large cats. The cats were content with the kills, although they eyed Brady's unit balefully. Once the dead animals were dragged away by the family of cats, the unit hustled ahead to replenish their water containers from the lake. It was pristine, with crystal-clear, cold water. There were fish visible, swimming about.

"Do you think this is safe to drink?" asked Misty.

"We have no choice but to risk it. We can't dally around. We go around the lake and keep moving south. Hopefully, the fish are safely edible too."

"What's to the south?" asked Sara.

"We'll find out when we get there."

Rather than look at judgmental and skeptical faces, Brady merely walked away. Leadership had never been something he sought. Now it had been thrust upon him, as none of the others chose to lead. In reality, he was the highest ranking of the enlisted troops, so he was the leader by default anyway.

The unit automatically resumed their configuration with Bontag at point again. In essence, it was another default choice. Bontag was best equipped for that job by physiology, skills, and experience. The large eyes and ears on his smooth, green-tinged head gave him senses and perceptions heightened above those of humans and the other species in the corps. Also, his lean, somewhat-spindly body could glide over terrain without the impact of far heavier beings, like Jocol. Ferreting out traps and dangers was a skill innate with Bontag the others could only covet.

As they moved, Brady pondered their desperate situation, trying to anticipate problems in advance. However, they'd been on the ground for such a short duration, they had no real experiences to aid them on this planet.

As they moved toward a sparser area of woodlands, they increased their caution and vigilance. They used Bontag as a bellwether, allowing him to trudge ahead; if he couldn't uncover hidden hazards, none of them could.

Nearing a mountain chain where the ground ascended sharply, Bontag stopped and looked back at them.

Brady pondered whether to skirt the mountains and stay on lower ground, but he had no basis for a choice either way.

"Bontag, what do you think?"

Bontag looked upward. "The forest continues up the mountain sides, so we'd still have cover. It would be more difficult ground for any pursuers trying to follow us."

"Lead the way."

Starting their steep ascent, it wasn't long before they were huffing and puffing with the exertion, which came right after the terrible battle and the rapid pace running to escape. Being in prime physical shape was no guarantee that they wouldn't be tested in the variety of hostile environments they would face on various planets. Stopping for a brief respite, water, and another food packet, they rested briefly. Fortunately, drinking the lake water had caused no problems.

"I haven't seen any signs of enemy troops in the area. There are no visible fortified buildings, camps, or other signs that this is an active zone of control." Brady glanced at Misty, who was seated beside him. Her face still mirrored her concern.

"Good," Misty replied. "I've seen those killers as much as I care to. Drawing notice to our position, we don't need that."

"What's our status with ammo?" asked Brady.

"We could have about one sustained firefight before we're tapped out."

"I guess we need another Plan B."

"Fighting those things without our weapons is not realistic."

"I know, Misty, and yet that's where we are. We need to come up with a solution—and in a hurry."

Again, their rest was a brief one. Following Bontag, they continued their trek up the mountain. It was rugged terrain and a difficult ascent, and there was no clear path to follow. Instead, they often forced their way through thorny thickets and brambles. Clinging vines didn't help either. They were thankful for the genius who had invented the special fabric of their combat uniforms, which provided protection from nearly any danger, whether the thorns, which couldn't penetrate the fabric, or other hazards, like poison from any plants. Additionally, they were kept warm, or cool, whatever was needed, with a built-in, automatic, self-regulating, rheostat-control device that adapted to the physiology of any species.

Stopping mid-afternoon for a brief meal, rest, and relief, Brady once again pondered his options, which at that point were nothing at all. As was the case on this planet, a storm moved in quickly. One minute they were sitting under a clear sky, and then the next moment, massive, roiling, multi-colored clouds darkened the sky from horizon to horizon. Crackling, jagged bolts of lightning, along with booms of thunder, swept over the little group. It was an apocalyptic sight and particularly frightening, since they were caught out in the open. On this planet, it was doubly terrifying, as the wind blowing through the heavy forest sounded like the approach of a feral tidal wave. The fury of the wind storm hit, causing them all to hunker down, grasping anything solid to maintain their positions, which was followed by a drenching downpour that pounded them mercilessly. It was more than just the discomfort of being rained upon. The ground quickly became slick and muddy, which made footing dangerous on such slanted ground.

"Bontag, what do you think?"

"I can make it, but it will be very slow going, Brady. For the rest of you, I don't know. We should probably wait it out."

"Maybe we try to find a better perch? It's dicey if we stay here."

"Okay, I'll check, but you should definitely remain here while I search."

Although Brady was reluctant to separate his forces, there seemed to be no other way.

"Bontag, you be very careful. We can afford zero mistakes."

"I understand. You can trust me."

He slipped away while the others watched in concern. It was easy to feel vulnerable, and Bontag's critical importance to the survival of the group couldn't be underestimated. He was gone for too long a time for their liking, but finally he came back.

"We were getting worried," said Misty. She gave Bontag a hug, a departure from her normal serious and detached demeanor about battle situations.

It surprised Bontag. He smiled at her. "Thank you, but I said you could trust me."

Turning his head to Brady, he explained, "There was no place close, but I did find a possibility farther up. It appears to be a cave mouth, although I didn't go in to explore it. At least we'd have some measure of protection from the elements, and possibly a new home."

"Okay, that sounds good. Can we make it there in this rain?"

"It was difficult for me, so I'd say we stay here through the storm and make the climb after it stops. Meanwhile, we can take care of our personal hygiene needs and wash up, since we have this free shower."

Everybody chuckled.

"Whatever," Brady replied.

Concerns of modesty had long ago disappeared in the corps. Showering together was normal and routine, so an unclad member of the opposite sex was seen as no big deal. The risk of some people attempting to take liberties was curbed by very strong penalties.

After cautiously washing their bodies in stages on their precarious perch, everybody felt better at being somewhat cleansed.

"Thank you, Brady. I hate to be grungy. That's always one of the bad parts of being in combat," said Sara.

"You're welcome. I aim to please."

The rain continued unabated for hours. Therefore, the terrible footing got even worse. Sitting in place became a test.

In addition to the soggy soil loosening under the deluge, it was covered by leaves and other accumulated foliage detritus, and also some scree, mixed in the soil, which made the ground even more hazardous.

"Damn it," Jocol muttered. Being the largest of them, he was the most at risk of starting to slide down the incline.

Brady made a command decision. "Let's go up to that cave, folks. We crawl if we must. Sitting here isn't working."

As if it was punishment from the planet for the sin of their presence, the moment they started to move upwards, the rain became worse, pelting them ferociously. In fact, they were reduced to crawling, all but Bontag. He managed to ambulate on the difficult terrain, as if he was glued to the ground, incapable of slipping.

Predictably, Jocol had the most trouble. Even with crawling, he slipped often and had to claw his way along.

"I'm going to need another bath," he huffed.

"Hang in there, everybody," Brady replied. "A nice cozy cave awaits us."

"I can hardly wait," Misty added.

The fury of the storm reached a peak, and then suddenly the rain abated to a mist.

"Thank God," Brady whispered.

Their trek was still hazardous, but one of the impediments had been reduced. It was still slow going, though, and it took a long time to make their way to a vantage point where they could see the cave for the first time.

"Hello, beautiful," said Jocol. The unit chuckled.

Forging ahead, they scaled the remaining distance before approaching the mouth of the cave. It was totally dark, like looking into a tunnel, so they had no way to gauge the natural formation, if it was shallow or deep. Pausing long enough to get all five of them into the entrance, Brady glanced into the gloom.

"Well, I guess it serves no purpose to delay. Bontag, use your light so we don't stumble off a cliff or something."

Bontag moved away, going around a curve with the unit arrayed in single file behind him. Ahead of them was continuous darkness. Inching along in silence, they were wary. It was the normal state of elite combat troops, being prepared for anything.

Brady most worried this was the abode of predators, but that didn't prove to be the case. As they moved into an open area, they were suddenly surrounded and bathed in light from torches held by warriors who brandished primitive weapons, such as spears, war clubs, bows and arrows, and so forth. These were not the same enemy troops the corps had been fighting. Halting, Brady pondered for only a moment before making another command decision. Holstering his weapon, he put up his hands and stepped forward to approach the male that appeared to be in charge.

These weren't the huge, daunting, enemy warriors. Instead, they were smaller, more normal in size, and a slightly different species of humanoids, very similar to the humans in the corps. Brady spoke through another miracle of their technology, a universal translator. He communicated with the warrior chieftain. "I'm Brady. We come in peace."

"What? You speak our tongue? How is that possible? Are you gods?"

"Eh . . . no, we're not gods. We're soldiers from other worlds."

"We saw you war with the Urghurs."

"Urghurs, is that their name?"

"Yes, they're also from off-world. We lived in peace and harmony before they came from the sky to conquer us. We had no weapons against such might and were a peaceful people. Although we cheered any progress you made in slaughtering them, we weren't sure if you were worse than they are. Do you understand?"

"I do understand. So, are you the indigenous species on this world?"

"Yes, this was our world all the way back to the beginning of time. We were content to live in peace with each other and our environment. That all changed radically with their coming. We were forced to learn battle instantly. Never had we seen such brutality. At times, the Urghur slaughtered for no other reason than that they could. We could only hide and move about to avoid their search. We extracted some small revenge as we came upon small groups of them, but that was rare, and ultimately it accomplished nothing."

"I'm sorry that happened to you."

"I believe you. Although you could be filled with guile to mislead us, I think you are true in what you say. I will take the risk to trust you, stranger."

"Thank you. We appreciate this very much."

"Come with me. I'll introduce you to my people."

Misty edged over. "Do you think we can trust them?"

"I'm just happy they're willing to trust us. We don't really have another option. We need all the help we can get."

Chapter Two

As they moved forward in the cave, Brady realized how many warriors were present as they followed the chief down the winding tunnel. Literally, it was an army.

"What are you called?" asked the chief.

"If you're asking about our races, me and the two women are humans. Jocol, the big guy, is a Gartan, and Bontag is a Vessian. My name is Brady, the black-haired woman is Misty, and the blondish woman is Sara."

"Thank you, Brady. Sharing your names is important to my people. There is power in a name, and trust is very important to us. We are called the Akara, which in our language means 'first people.' As I said, we were here to see the first sunrise on this world."

"That's amazing."

"What brought you to our world, Brady?"

"I wish I could tell you we had some noble goal, but the five of us are mere soldiers following the orders of our superiors. What their plan was, what drew them here, I can't tell you, because I don't know."

"You're honest, even when the truth is difficult. This helps me to understand your true character and aids me a great deal in judging you."

"We're here in your cave because we were driven away by the enemy. Most of our army retreated back to the fleet in space. We were part of the rear guard defending the retreat. The escape window closed before we could leave, so basically, we're marooned here. To my knowledge, there were about a hundred of us left. To survive, we fanned out in five-person units to go undercover on the run. I don't know about the other departure points across this globe if there were other troops marooned."

"I think your army did great damage to the enemy. We believe they call themselves the Kralc, though what the distinction is from Urghur, we don't know. I'm not even sure where that name and idea came from. The Akara only call them Urghur, which means 'the soulless' in our language. Though they've been on our world for a very long time, we know little about them, other than they're traveling marauders who go from world to world, slaying and destroying.

"I think my people were seen as food, as they consume us. And they're sending many Akara captives away on their ships, I think as a food source for their home world. They're a vile scourge and do no good in the universe. If we had the power, we would wipe them out completely. This is why I say thankfully you've killed huge numbers of them. However, we haven't ventured out to test that theory yet."

"I wish we could you help in wiping them out completely, but stranded here, we can't resupply either our food or ammo."

"Ammo?"

"Think of your arrows as ammo. If you fired all of your arrows and had no way to replenish them, that's how it is for us."

"I see. So at this point, you're also helpless against their might. That is sad to hear, my new friend."

"The only possible solution I can think of is if we begin to kill off their soldiers, we take their weapons. Obviously, we'd need to do that a little at a time, but gradually we'd start to build up a modern weapons cache. It would help to even the odds for our side in future fights."

"We have taken weapons from their dead, but we knew nothing about them. There's a large collection of their weapons here in the cave."

"That's great news."

"Listen, I must explain that I have accepted you and extended my trust, but ultimate power in our society resides in the high council. I will speak for you before them, but the final decision is theirs."

"I understand, and that's fair. We appreciate whatever you can do."

"I am named Rosca, chief of my people here. There are other clans with their own chiefs all across this world."

"I hope we can prove to be good friends for the Akara."

"As I said, I trust you. That is a big thing."

They completed the descent along the tunnel, which expanded in size the farther along they went. Reaching the bottom, they were ushered into a vast cavern and a huge makeshift city of huts. The largest building was in the center of the huts. Considerable guards surrounded that structure. Although flickering light from torches illuminated the city, there was an ancient, natural, volcanic fissure overhead that provided light from the surface, an outlet for campfire smoke to escape upwards and ventilation of fresh air. It was a perfect abode for the large collection of Akara citizenry.

Rosca explained as they neared the center, pointing at the large main building, "It is our holy sanctuary. Do not speak at this time. Leave it to me."

Approaching the solid line of fierce and angry-looking guards, they challenged their own chief, hands on weapons.

"Halt. Why do you bring strangers to this divine place? Are you compelled by them?" They drew out their weapons, including swords, and assumed defensive stances.

"I ask to speak to the holy council. These strangers stand before you as my guests. I take full responsibility for them and their actions."

"Our charge is to protect the council, to the death. None may pass who are not of the blood of the people."

Rosca frowned at the adamant stares of his own warriors.

The captain of the guard continued, "Taking the cause of these enemy soldiers before the council is an outrage and is a sacrilege."

"Your charge was given to you by me, your chief." Rosca eyed the belligerent captain grimly. "I vouch for these guests. Take my life or stand aside."

For a moment, Brady feared the guards would attack their own leader. The captain glowered and stood a moment, considering rash action, before finally he relented, admitting the chief into the holy hut. But he stepped close to Brady and put his sword tip against Brady's chest.

Brady was irked, and the captain saw it in his eyes. "Make your move, fool. You will die before you can flinch."

Brady shrugged and took a step back.

The captain smirked. "So, you are cowards. How does the chief think you're helpful to the Akara?"

Brady turned his back to the affront, looked at Misty, and smiled. "So, are you okay?"

"Sure. We've got your back, boss." She eyed the Akara captain grimly, her hand resting on her weapon in her holster.

Jocol took a slight step toward the captain and his expression was deadly. He towered over everyone.

"Perhaps you wish to call me cowardly?"

The captain seethed, but wisely, he took no action. It was clear to everybody Jocol was not a person to tamper with. With him, there would be a deadly fight if the needless posturing continued.

25

To avoid a mistake, Brady moved his unit back away from the line, where they assumed non-threatening postures, and relaxed and chatted among themselves. Consuming swallows of water and a food packet each, they acted as if there was no danger here.

Meanwhile, huge crowds of curious citizens gathered to stare at the strangers in their midst. After ages of fear of the Urghur menace, tolerating the presence of strangers among them was a novelty.

The unit members saw Akara children for the first time, although the parents grabbed them from trying to approach the five. Jocol, in particular, commanded the most attention. He ignored them and chatted with his comrades.

Suddenly, one brash little girl slipped out of her mother's hold and hustled up to the E3T troops. Brady turned, knelt down to her, and smiled.

"Hi, little one, how are you today?"

The assembled throng gasped as she quickly went into his embrace for a hug. He caressed her gently, before releasing her as the mother cautiously approached.

"Pardon me, stranger. My daughter is too . . ." She didn't finish her sentence.

Brady smiled at the woman. "Ma'am, I want to thank you for allowing me to meet her. She's truly a treasure beyond measure. I'm honored."

That brought a smile to her face. "Come, Liara."

"I want to stay."

"Enough with your disobedience; come with me this minute."

The episode changed the mood in the cavern. Suddenly, the unit wasn't seen in terms of the savage Urghur horde; they were now benign new friends. Even the belligerence in the guard captain faded away.

The unit resumed their friendly posture. No other children approached them, however, as the other parents remained cautious.

The chief pleading their case before the council was a much longer session than the unit anticipated. Whether that was good or bad, they had no way to know.

Food was taken into the council chamber after hours of waiting.

None of the city residents chose to leave. They were curious about the decision of the council also.

It was difficult to gauge the passage of time down in a cave without being able to see the movement of the sun. Other than their own wristwatches, it would have been nearly impossible to know. After another lengthy delay, at last Rosca emerged from the meeting, accompanied by the entire council. The fact the crowd gasped when they saw them told the unit members this wasn't usual procedure.

"My friends, are you well?"

"We are, Rosca, thank you. Again, we appreciate your help."

"I explained your situation to my brothers on the council as best I could. I hope I did you no disservice through my ignorance of your world and your ways. Suffice to say, there was resistance in the brothers, much resistance. The actions of the Urghur cast a long shadow over any visitors to our world. For them to believe you can have pure motives was … well … challenging. I suggested they meet you to assess for themselves. Please understand, this is a huge departure from our normal ways. The council members are holy and aren't normally seen by the populace, and certainly not by strangers. However, these are trying times that call for new ways to approach things. They finally agreed this was the best path."

"What do we say or do?"

"They will speak to each of you separate from the others. Is that acceptable?"

"Sure, no problem."

Turning his head to the unit, Brady asked, "Did you guys hear that?"

"Yes," they replied in unison.

"We've got this, Brady," said Misty.

The five moved apart and were immediately approached by various council members, and the conversations began.

Rosca stayed initially with Brady, but then went to each of the other unit members, monitoring the discussions.

The Akara were particularly fascinated with the two human female soldiers. Females had different roles in Akara society, which didn't include defending their people. They were slighter in stature compared to humans, and to see these two superb human women fighters, who were physically fit to the maximum, with perfect physiques, confident, and imposing in their countenance, was fascinating in a lot of ways. For the women, realizing they were irresistibly alluring to the Akara males, they eyed Brady mirthfully at the circus atmosphere they created. Neither woman had sought celebrity in her life. Now here they were in that very situation.

The only tense moment came when a particularly avid, curious, and admiring young warrior made the poor choice to touch Misty in the wrong place. She reacted like a coiled spring, snatching his hand into a painful twist, but she stopped short of injuring the foolish young male.

"Dude, you don't touch those unless you want to lose some fingers."

The captain intervened, yanking the offending soldier away, shaking him and whispering at him angrily. A council member spoke. "We sincerely beg your pardon. Young men can be rambunctious."

"I understand, sir. No offense taken. I'll assume it's a lesson learned. Let's forget it ever happened."

"Thank you for your forbearance. Obviously, the ways of your people are much different than our ways."

"That would be true."

"You are a wonder for us, you and your sister."

"She's not literally my sister, but we are sisters-in-arms."

"The chief is correct; these are different times calling for different solutions."

The council members gathered back together, whispering for a time. Finally, they called in the chief to deliver their ruling.

Rosca turned to address the assemblage. "My friends, the council has accepted my recommendations. Please welcome our new friends into the community of the Akara. I vouch for them all and state they are trustworthy and no danger to the people."

It set off a spontaneous cheer from the throng, followed by the people closing in to speak and touch the unit members. It was comical to see enormous Jocol surrounded by a mass of children. Lifting armloads of them like they were weightless, their parents laughed at the spectacle of this gentle giant. Obviously, they'd never seen him in battle.

Second most popular, predictably, were the two human women. Their admirers weren't the children; it was the young warriors, though they'd learned the hard lesson of appropriate boundaries.

Rosca approached Brady. "We will house you in the city for this night. Tomorrow, with your permission, can we talk further about our joint future path? If you are truly stranded here, this is your home and you must make provision for that fact."

"Agreed."

"Do you stay together? We don't know your ways. Do you have family situations, like we marry, to have families?"

"Back home, we all come from families and have parents. In the army, none of us here are married. Though we stay together, it's not on an intimate basis between us. I think we all planned on getting married at some point in time and having families later. If there is a hut large enough for all of us, that's fine. Otherwise, whatever arrangements you make, we can cope."

"I'll set some people to work on it right away. We'll have something worked out before we sleep tonight."

"Thank you, Rosca, and thank you again for trusting us. I know you took a huge leap of faith, so I want you to know that we won't let you down."

"That's good to hear, my human friend."

Later, Rosca returned. "I regret to tell you, we don't have an open hut large enough to house all of you, so we decided to build one. Obviously, that will take a little time. In the meantime, if this is agreeable, each of you will be housed with a host family. The people love this choice, and we've been flooded with requests to be the hosts. What do you say about that?"

"That's fine."

"Do you wish to pick them?"

"No, I'll leave it to you. I have no basis to pick one over another."

"So be it. I'll make the choices."

Later, at the time to retire for sleep, the unit gathered with Rosca. It was mildly entertaining to see the glee on the faces of the host families, like they'd won the lottery.

Brady turned to Jocol. "Wait until they get a dose of your snoring. The bloom will be off the rose in a hurry."

The unit members laughed, but Jocol scowled.

It was a fascinating process for Brady to watch as the unit was allocated. Jocol went to a family with a large number of children.

They cheered and gathered around him in an impromptu mass hug, as he looked on in bewilderment.

It amused Brady to notice the crack in Jocol's normally gruff exterior. Accolades had never been a part of his life, and certainly no hero worship. Sensing Brady's amused stare, he turned his face to glower at him.

Next, Bontag was sent to another family with children. With him, he was pleased and smiled warmly at the positive attention.

Sara went to a family with all sons. They'd eyed her adoringly. Looking at Brady, she shook her head in helplessness at the cow-eyed looks of adolescent adoration.

Misty went to a large family where the daughters worshipped her as much as the sons. Equally agog, the sons wanted to marry her, and the daughters wanted to be her.

Lastly, Brady joined a family of daughters, some nearly grown. Seeing the same avid expressions on their faces, Brady had no problem recognizing that romantic thoughts were bouncing around in their adolescent brains.

"Hello," he said to the father.

"We're honored to open our door to you. I think a new day has begun for our people. Perhaps we can have hope in our lives."

"I share your hopes for better days, sir."

"I'm Bren. This is my wife Sala, and my daughters, Beca, Sira, Wyla, Miran, and Senni."

"Hello, ladies."

Sala had a warm smile, while her daughters' tee-heed and snickered together, eyeing Brady like he was dessert for the evening meal. The exception was Beca, the oldest, and a woman in every sense. Brady was also unfamiliar with being in the spotlight. Being a teen's heartthrob wasn't his first choice for passing his time among the Akara.

"Our home is this way. Please come with me."

A prominent family, their hut wasn't far from the ceremonial center of the city. Once they went inside, it wasn't particularly large. He'd be living in close quarters, and the thought of causing an incident with some unknowing blunder of one of their rules worried him.

"Is something wrong? Is our home not acceptable?"

"Your home is fine. In close quarters, I just don't want to do something to upset you."

The Akara family laughed. Bren said, "Don't worry about that. This is a high honor for us being chosen as a host family."

"Okay, but be sure to warn me about any mistakes I'm about to make, please. It's a high honor for me to be hosted."

"I could say the same. My daughters are . . . well . . . typical young ladies, full of ideas."

"Don't worry about that. I think the more I'm around them, the less they'll be enamored."

"I do not think so," said Sala. "They dream big of adventure and life as the wife of a great war hero."

"The great war hero idea is a stretch, and that would not be me. Trust me; they can do much better."

Bren and Sala smiled at him and then at each other.

Sala spoke, "How strange this is after the life we've lived at the mercy of the Urghurs, constantly racing about to avoid hideous death. You don't understand that for us, you represent hope where there was none."

"There are only five of us here, and a total of a hundred survivors worldwide that I'm aware of. You realize we didn't really defeat the Urghurs."

"Allow us our dreams, even if they might be short-lived."

"Sure, no problem, folks. What I can say is we're your friends. We're willing to die defending you."

Both parents got glassy-eyed looks.

Bren spoke to Sala. "I told you their coming was a good omen."

They embraced while their five daughters stood nearby, eyeing Brady. Again, he felt like a steak about to be served up for dinner. In a way, it was a more daunting moment than going into battle for him. Looking around, there was only the one large room.

Bren explained. "We share all of life in our society. Is that a problem? Do you live separately?"

"I'm fine. Where do I sleep?"

"You will be placed between my wife on your right and my daughters on your left. Is that acceptable?"

"Sure. Is it the same for my comrades in the other houses?"

"Yes."

Brady smiled.

"What is funny?"

"Whoever got Jocol is going to be introduced to the concept of snoring."

"What is that?"

"During his sleep, he makes a great deal of noise."

"Is it dangerous?"

"Only for your ears and a good night of rest."

"Then we're doubly blessed," said Sala. "I think it's good for the people to experience different peoples and different practices. Is this snoring a good thing?"

"I very much doubt that."

"Oh."

"Perhaps we will have a meal before it's time to sleep?" asked Sala, eyeing Brady meekly.

"Do whatever you normally do, folks. Don't try to cater to me. Soldiers spend their lives coping, so doing your normal habits won't be a problem for me."

"You're kind to say these things. I know our simple life must be silly to you with the active, adventurous kind of life you live."

"Actually, your simple style of life has great appeal for us. You understand coping with fear because you've lived it. We go from battle to battle, never knowing what to expect each time. The end can come at any time as a soldier. Living with fear and stress is one of the first hurdles for us to conquer in the army. Believe me when I say it's not easy."

Sala looked sad. Turning away, she muttered as she went to start the meal. The older daughters joined her while the younger ones sat in awe of Brady.

"So, do you girls go to school?" he asked, smiling at their small, dainty faces.

"All of us are with the tutors except Beca, who is oldest. She's now of an age to consider a mate," Senni, the youngest, responded.

"I see. What do you learn from the tutors?"

"We're taught the history of the people, girls learn the skills needed about food, rearing children, laws, the rules of proper conduct, and so forth. There are many topics, and it varies with the pupil. We're guided as we show aptitudes for certain skills. Some assist the healers, some teach, some care for the injured and sick, some of the braver are given more dangerous tasks outside the safety of the caves. When the hunters go afield, women can join them to help with the kills, harvesting the meat quickly for rapid movement back to safety. With the danger of predators, compounded by Urghur patrols, it takes certain kinds of people to do that."

"They're very brave young women."

Bren smiled. "They've given you the briefest of answers. There is far more to the education of the young."

"I can believe that. Children are the future. Nothing can be more important than that."

"By necessity, since the horror of the Urghurs coming, we, as a people, have hunkered down in hiding to avoid the dangers. Some settlements aren't lucky. Although we relocate, occasionally the enemy comes upon us in our lairs, trapping us. It's ... terrible ... as you can imagine. You've seen what they do."

"I have. It gave us great rage in fighting them."

The meal was served soon afterwards. Beca insisted on personally serving Brady his food.

"Is this acceptable?" she asked in a dainty voice, smiling demurely.

"It is. Thank you for your kindness, Beca."

"If you need anything further, just ask me."

"I've got all that I need; thanks."

She sat down beside him. "May I ask you, those women, Misty and Sara, are they your mates?"

"No, we really can't afford to have mates in wars. As a combat soldier, if you had your wife with you and were worried about her and not paying attention to your job, it could get you both killed. Do you understand?"

"I do understand. It seems unfair to impose this on you. How can you have your life?"

"It's a choice we make, Beca. The army is a job that needs to be done, but that doesn't mean it is fair. We've chosen to be the defenders for our people, with the idea that someday we'll move on to the next phase of life."

"It seems such a waste of good lives."

"It is that, I can't disagree, but think about your enemies, the Urghur. They're merciless, pitiless brutes bereft of normal emotions. Someone must stand up against them. That's why you have your soldiers."

"You're right. I wonder, though, what can I do about this trouble? I'm just a female."

"Beca, there's no such thing as just a female. Women are a treasure beyond measure and the center of the lives of men. Not every society looks at women like your people do. I think that's an area the Akara can improve upon."

The looks he got from all the females present at that point, regardless of age, abject adoration, momentarily floored him. He worried Beca was about to jump on him on the spot in her overwhelming display of excitement.

"I probably sound like an idiot."

Sala replied. "No, you don't sound like an idiot, Brady. For us, you're the treasure."

He shrugged self-consciously and glanced at Bren, who had a rueful smile.

"With my nattering, I'm going to give you all brain damage."

The entire family laughed heartily.

Beca spoke. "I wish we could freeze this moment in time. This is special." She eyed him longingly, as did her sisters. "Is there anything more you would like?"

"No, I'm good, Beca."

The family readied to sleep soon after cleaning up from the meal. Lying between Sala on one side and Beca on the other side was an experience. Beca lay on her side, facing him, and stared. Brady closed his eyes quickly to put it out of his mind. She was a pretty, appealing young woman, with brown hair, brown eyes, and angelic, delicate facial features.

He smiled at the thought of his comrades facing their own challenges with Akara family adoration. As usual for combat troops, falling asleep came quickly.

He woke up the following day when the family got up. Feeling fully rested was another luxury they did without in the field. After a quick breakfast, a surprisingly diverse meal with meat, fruits, cheese, vegetables, and a delicious fruit-based drink, Brady went out with Bren to join his E3T comrades and their hosts.

Rosca smiled. "Greetings, my friends, you all seem to be well."

"It was nice of those families to host all of us."

"Today, if you're agreeable, perhaps we can talk about plans?"

"That's exactly what I'd like to do. I want to contact our other units to determine their situations. I'd like for you to stand by, because the others may not have run into your people or found places of safety to stay. In case there is trouble, perhaps you can speak to your people on our behalf?"

"I don't understand. How could I do that?"

"With these devices, we can talk over distances. I suspect the Urghurs must do this also. At any rate, if my comrades can get chiefs of those other settlements to speak directly with you, maybe we can speed up the process. Once all of my people are safe, embedded in local communities, we can formulate more plans to take more actions."

"I'm agreeable to this. You're full of marvels. We haven't seen the Urghurs with such devices that talk over distance."

"It's simply one of many technological developments we've accomplished. As far as the Urghur, maybe they have some other method."

"Techno ..."

"Technology. It has its good side and its bad side. You've seen how the Urghurs use it for bad purposes with their weapons."

"That I understand."

"Anyway, let me see if I can raise our troops, so we can get this show on the road."

"Huh? What does that mean?"

"It's a figure of speech. Don't worry about it."

It took half an hour before they linked every unit into the joint connection. Brady explained the situation and his plan. Most of the other units were still exposed and in jeopardy. Several had run into the Akara, although both sides merely eyed each other warily. Joining into the joint communication, Rosca was fascinated talking to his brethren far away. Agreements were quickly struck, and unit by unit, E3T moved underground into safe havens. Those units still afar were directed where to go to find shelter and allies. By the next day, all of the hundred survivors were out of imminent danger.

Chapter Three

A new day had dawned for the Akara people. E3T had entered their lives, and now more than just one settlement felt hope. The fulfillment of that hope would depend on the plans they made and, to an extent, the status of the enemy. On their next joint *communiqué*, Brady solicited observations from everywhere, asking what each Akara community had noticed locally after the battles.

Uniformly, he heard a similar theme.

"The patrols of the Urghur are greatly reduced in frequency, and when we see them, they're far smaller in numbers. Also, they seem restrained, for them, compared to how voracious they were before. I think your bombs wiped out a great many of them after your army fled."

"That would be very good news. Have the others of you noticed the same things?"

"Yes." There were none who disagreed with the observation.

"If we go on the assumption they're weakened, perhaps we should start reconnaissance runs to fully assess their battle readiness and locate their camps."

One of the other chiefs from across the planet made a comment. "I would like to tell you, we have a community member who is brilliant, far above the rest of us. His name is Visule, which comes from our word for 'visionary.' Perhaps he's on an intellectual par with your people? Regardless, he tells me he's studied the Urghur from afar for decades, and he believes they're unique in a certain way. They operate like some insects, like a swarm, but function as a single entity. In their case, he believes they have a mental connection, a single mass consciousness. Whatever happens to one individual, they're all simultaneously aware of it. If we attack a patrol, or even one of them, they will all know of it instantly. Obviously, it will cause a response, and they'll know where to go at that point."

"Interesting," Brady replied. "Has your man been able to discern any language?"

"They don't need to speak verbally with their sharing of thoughts. Equally, they don't speak to victims whom they immediately kill and consume for food."

"That would seem to imply there must be a queen somewhere. I wonder how far that mental connection extends. Is it limited to planetary vicinities, or does it go out into space to whatever vessels they use to travel between planets?"

"I understand what you're asking. If we attack them, are we alerting just the swarm on this planet, or all Urghur everywhere in the universe?"

"Exactly. With these communicators of ours, we can't contact our own fleet once they leave orbit around this world. I'd hope that's also true for our enemy. If it's just us against whatever is left of them, I like our chances much better. It means making the first move is the critical one, because we're not sure what comes afterwards in terms of Urghur retaliation."

"We trust whatever you decide. You're far more qualified to make the choice than any of us."

"I hope you're right. None of us are officers. We didn't make the battlefield decisions in our army."

"Regardless, you tell us what we should do, and we'll do it as best we can. We of the Akara will no longer live under the boot of the Urghur butchers."

"Okay, my decision is we all send out recon patrols, so if there is contact and conflict, they can't center on one specific place. If they try to dispatch forces to all of the ambush sites, obviously their forces will be diluted and subsequently weakened. At that point, we take them down and capture their weapons. With each win, more of our forces are armed with modern weapons, which is one of our first goals. We need to be able to fight them on an equal footing."

"We agree with this plan. One other observation which Visule wants to share is the Urghur show one other facet, a disturbing fact. They seem to be cognizant of our ways, feelings, societal structure, and so forth. There have been numerous examples of purposeful cruelty. For instance, capturing victims like family groups to consume, but slaughtering them in designated ways, such as making parents watch their children being eaten before their eyes to relish their anguish and heartbreak before killing those parents. Making the husband watch his wife be killed, or vice versa. Do you understand what we're getting at? They have a malicious streak in addition to the other bad aspects of their natures. Delighting in the torment of their victims seems to be an appalling entertainment for them, unless there is some other reason we don't comprehend."

"That is sickening. Attacking your spirits would seem to be their goal. Send out forces at first light tomorrow morning. Load the strike teams with overwhelming numbers. For all E3T personnel, this is it. No failures tolerated. Kill them all to the last man. Rearm with their weapons too. If you locate their camps, send word, and we'll organize an attack plan accordingly."

"Yes sir, General Brady Black."

"Very funny, idiots."

Brady heard chuckles from all of the other comm units.

"Listen, guys, I didn't ask for this."

"Brady, we're joking."

"Brady out." Cutting them off, he was perturbed, not at the troops, but at the revelation about Urghur cruelties.

He looked at his little crew smirking at him. He shook his head mirthfully. "Jarheads, they never change. There's really nothing else people like us can do as a job. We're all idiots, and I'm at the head of that line."

"Hey, speak for yourself," Misty replied, smiling.

"You just happen to be a very pretty idiot, Misty."

"Okay, dumb ass! Don't forget I can bring the pain, dude."

Brady laughed and ducked, trying to avoid her playful swat. Beca was standing close by, observing this human behavior with keen interest. Banter wasn't something she saw in Akara society, especially the equal footing between males and females. It amused and intrigued her.

In his time living in the underground city, Brady had noticed that wherever he went, he tended to see Beca. It wasn't hard to put those puzzle pieces together.

Brady continued. "Anyway, we know what to do next, so everybody get your minds battle-ready. Tomorrow, we start to bring the pain to the Urghurs."

"Hoorah," said his E3T comrades.

Their martial chant caused amused looks among the Akara. Rosca spoke, "Please don't take our reaction wrong. We're entertained by your ways. It's a good lesson for us as we ponder making our own changes. There is much you can teach us. The old ways didn't work out too well for us with the challenges we faced."

"We're not much of an example to emulate. Trust me; we're as flawed as any other race. There is a great deal of your ways to retain. You're decent folks, and that's something for us to emulate."

"Thank you. Coming from a higher race, that's very gratifying."

"Rosca, we're not a higher race. As I said before, we've got advanced technology, but that can be taught. When it comes to personal character, I suspect the Akara win hands down. The more you're around us, the more you'll realize this."

"Brady, you say such wonderful things."

"I'm an idiot."

"What is this 'idiot' you keep saying?"

"It came from our distant past on our home world, Earth. When our doctors assessed lower intelligence individuals, they created classifications of idiots, imbeciles, and morons. I honestly don't know which one was which, as far as the most or least stupid. Sorry."

The unit members chuckled. Sara commented, "Whatever was the hierarchy, in E3T, we've got them all covered."

Everybody laughed at her joke.

She continued, "Can you say 'blockhead'?'"

Misty added. "Obviously, those three categories cover the males."

"One of these days . . ." Brady brandished his fist in mock outrage.

"Bring it on," Misty retorted. "We'll see who feels the pain."

"I like this," said Beca. "Women and men talking as equals, this is how things should be. I would like to join your army."

The five smiled at her. Brady replied, "Beca, it may seem glamorous from your point of view, but you have no idea about the difficulties of life as a soldier. In addition to the most rigorous training possible, where you must develop skills in killing, you're thrust into battles where you must find ways within yourself to cope with taking lives, seeing comrades killed, and following some orders you may not believe in. Not every person in charge is worthy to make such decisions. In a perfect world, those types would have no power. However, there are no perfect worlds. At least, I've never seen any in my travels. Do you understand?"

"Because I don't have your societal experiences doesn't mean I couldn't become competent. If I'm the first female of my race to achieve such distinction, how is that a bad thing? Will you train me?"

"Eh . . ."

"Very profound, Brady," said Misty.

"Misty, give me a break," he groused. He looked at Beca's parents, who had concerned looks on their faces.

Bren spoke, "We've never had female fighters. It's a scary proposition. However, Beca is of an age to make her own decisions about many things."

Beca smiled at Brady. One of her choices for her future life course was obvious to all as she eyed Brady longingly. Putting the pieces together in his mind, it seemed logical she thought achieving a status on par with Sara and Misty might mean her validation in Brady's eyes. He pondered setting her straight, but he opted to let the moment pass without embarrassing her.

Sara spoke, "What do you say, Misty? I have no problem with training Beca."

"Sure, I'm in."

Beca laughed and looked at her parents. Predictably, they looked on with dismay.

"Mama, this will be a miracle for Akara women. I will do this difficult thing."

Sala didn't bother responding. She eyed her daughter with skepticism.

Everybody looked at Brady, like he needed to sign off on the project.

Shrugging his shoulders, he replied, "Okay. Ladies, it's in your hands. Beca, I want to be sure you understand the corps is the absolute elite of military forces. There is no more difficult a task than meeting our impossible requirements. If you really intend to do this, what you'll go through will be torturous, to say the least. You're slight of stature at this point, so the ladies will need to build you up to minimum strength levels, and that won't be pleasant. You can still back away, and nobody will think less of you."

"I will not, and though you think I will fail, I declare to you I will not. I represent more than myself and my family, I represent my people. I will be the first."

"Good luck with it. I truly mean that."

"That's the spirit, Beca," said Misty. "You've got me fired up now."

Beca's sisters gathered around her in excitement. Nearby, others of her people looked on in shock at the unanticipated twist. Nobody thought Beca could achieve this daunting goal. Some felt she shouldn't even try. At that point, for those opinionated people, bigger roles for females in Akara society wasn't something they saw as a good thing.

Brady turned back to the unit. "Form up. We take fifty Akara warriors with us. We're taking Akara weapons too, and they'll carry those captured Urghur weapons. If we can win a fight without wasting our ammo, we do that. Any questions?"

"Can I come?" asked Beca.

"No," Brady replied in no uncertain terms.

She looked hurt.

"Beca, you're not ready to go into danger," Misty clarified. "Your time will come."

That returned the smile to her face.

"I'm brave too, Brady. You'll see."

"Sure." He glanced away from her piercing stare. "Let's go, folks. We've got work to do."

Emerging from the mouth of the cave into a bright day with a clear sky, Brady paused for a moment to survey the landscape. Rosca looked at him in curiosity at his pensive mood.

"Is there a problem, my friend?"

"No. The elevated view from here is breathtaking, an idyllic vista with the beauty of the lush forest for as far as the eye can see. It makes me imagine the Earth story of the Garden of Eden. The fact that horrible death awaits the unwary out there is a strange dichotomy for such a peaceful-looking scene. The clean, oxygen-rich air is so invigorating it makes you feel very good, but a Garden of Eden with a kicker."

"It's been our truth for countless ages, what life could be like if there were no Urghur here. We yearn for better days."

"Let's change it. It's time to get to work."

Rosca smiled.

The E3T unit, plus the handpicked Akara warriors, left the protection of the mountain cave and made their way down the slope. It was so much easier to travel without driving rainstorms, plus the Akara had provided makeshift small cleats, which could be adjusted to slip onto the boots of the unit members, that they used for secure footing. It took only a fraction of the time to make the descent and begin the search for their foes.

It was a rare cloudless sky, although a brisk day, as they trudged along, searching for their Urghur enemies. With significantly more animal traffic, it seemed the enemy must be strangely missing, since the voracious Urghur ate animals too.

After walking for many hours, they stopped for a break and to have a quick meal before resuming the search.

Brady sat down with the military leader of this Akara troop, Bralic, the main subsidiary to Rosca.

"Is this normal for them?"

"Not at all, Brady. For us, coming this far down the mountain in such numbers would draw their attention and would usually lead to a bad ending. I don't know where their camps are, but this absence of the Urghur soldiers moving about surprises me. It would be very nice if they were all killed off by your bombs."

"I doubt that's the case."

"Regardless, this is a much better omen than I could have hoped for."

"We'll see. I always plan for the worst so I'm ready for anything. They may have changed tactics and are setting ambushes and traps. We're going to need to be doubly vigilant."

"I agree. I must tell you, the warriors feel confident traveling with you. That has never been the case for us going into danger. Our necessary hunting trips for food were always fraught with terrible risk. We frequently took casualties on those forays."

"I hope we warrant your trust. We'll do our best."

"As will we, Brady."

"Bontag, how are the warriors doing that you're training for the job of taking point?"

"Very well, they're doing great. Most have natural skills, which will serve us well in the task ahead. I'm favorably impressed. Their only possible shortcomings might come in the fights themselves, with the disparity of physical size compared to the Urghur. We'll find that out later. How to fight larger foes is a skill we need to teach them."

Brady nodded. Glancing at Bralic, he could see fire was in his eyes at the thought of fighting the Urghur on an equal footing.

"Bralic, I'm comfortable that my unit has mastered the use of your weapons and is proficient. That will be our main tactic. We'll only use modern weapons if we must. Once we harvest more enemy weapons from their dead, all of us can change how we fight. Of course, that assumes we capture their camps to get their ammo. Otherwise their captured weapons will soon be useless to us."

"I look forward to that day when we are armed with modern weapons. Losing battles to the Urghur must end. Let them be the ones who live in terror from now on."

Brady smiled at Bralic.

Bralic mentioned softly and thoughtfully, "You think I'm a fool."

"No, I don't. I think you're incredibly brave, and I understand you've had enough of the abuse."

"In our lives, we've all seen such horrors done to dear friends, that no one is unchanged by the anger growing in our hearts. None were safe from the depredations. Even women and children fell to their fatal designs. It puts consuming hatred and rage in your heart and your soul, but we just never had a means to do anything meaningful about it before. Do you see?"

"I do."

"We won't put you in jeopardy with foolish actions."

"I know that. We'll handle this. Once you get the first fight under your belt, everything will go smoother, because you'll gain confidence and hone your skills."

"Can I ask you, what do you think about this silliness from Beca? The Akara don't have our women in our fighting forces. It isn't right."

"Bralic, it's a new day in a lot of ways. Can you say you don't trust Sara and Misty to pull their weight in battle?"

"That's different."

"Is it? How Beca will be coming out of training might just surprise you."

"I'll believe it when I see it. I could best her with the merest of effort."

"Now, of course, but she hasn't started the work yet. Give her a chance under the guidance of my ladies. I can't say she's a sure thing to make it, but I see real determination and guts in her. I wouldn't be surprised if she becomes one of the greatest Akara warriors in your history."

Bralic shook his head. "Could such a thing happen?"

Brady smiled. "Stay tuned, dude. She's got some serious goals. I'm not going to prejudge what she can accomplish."

"Then I will wait also. This brashness she shows, it's drawn the notice of all the males. Now they all want to be her mate."

Brady chuckled. "Good luck with that. She's got her own ideas, and I suspect they're unconventional."

"Do you mean with you? Is that something you would ever consider, bonding with one of our women?"

"I'm a soldier. Marriage isn't a path any members of my unit consider at this point. After we're done with the army, maybe then we settle down. I would have nothing against Beca, or any other of your women, but whether it's her coming after me, or one of your males going after Sara or Misty, there's probably no realistic chance of success for the reasons I've given. We have no prejudice against the Akara, because at this point we're still soldiers. That requires total focus on the job at hand, which is killing the enemy. It doesn't leave room for tenderness, children, and families."

"I understand. In your situation, perhaps I'd feel the same way. For the Akara, we must maintain our race, so we join together and birth our babies under trying circumstances because there is no other way. My people know of Beca's intentions to win you over, and honestly, there are mixed opinions about that, no offense."

"None taken."

"Thank you. We greatly value this alliance and will do nothing to put it in jeopardy."

"Bralic, we need you a lot more than you need us. You've got no worries about stepping on our toes."

"This bond I feel with you and your comrades, it's unlike anything we have among the Akara. Here, as I said, I feel like we can accomplish anything. Those Urghur monsters that terrified us to near inaction, suddenly they don't frighten me."

"Well, they're the same threats, so we use necessary caution so we don't compound more tragedies. One last thing I want to explain to further clarify our positions, in our confederation, intermarriage between races is common enough. We don't reject any Akara romantic advances for any other reasons than what I've told you; for the practical side of it. Your people are as appealing as potential mates as any other race to us."

"I understand and thank you."

"Are you ready?"

"Yes, let's continue."

Bontag took the lead, along with his new protégés. The mixed unit of allies formed up behind them and moved out in single file. As always, Jocol brought up the rear; however, he too had his set of protégés, the huskiest of the Akara warriors. To them, he was like a god, a mammoth, intimidating being of muscle and might.

Traveling into sparser areas where the concealing trees thinned, still there were no Urghur soldiers to be found. Additionally, they expected no help from Urghur cooking fires to help find them, because the Urghur didn't cook their kills; they ate them raw, and usually while they were still alive.

Looking upward frequently, Brady never saw or heard any signs of air traffic. Whether that meant allied forces had annihilated all Urghur aircraft, they'd fled the planet, or possibly were cached somewhere, he had no way to know. An enemy air force could be a game changer.

Certainly, whatever link they'd had to transport living victims back to their home world seemed to have ended. The determined Akara nation was no longer going to be an entrée for Urghur dinner tables, one way or another.

Bontag cautiously led them across a clearing. Before they could go into the forest across the way, they met their quarry. Urghur cries sounded ahead of them, and soon enemy troops emerged, charging in their typical attack frenzy. What was different this time was the lack of overwhelming numbers.

Deploying according to a prearranged array, the allies opened up with Akara weapons, arrows, spears, and then, in close-quarter fighting, with swords, war hammers, and cudgels. Even with the physical power of the Urghur fighters, Jocol was a titan, felling enemy troops like he was harvesting wheat, knocking them down like bowling pins. This inspired the Akara, who threw themselves into the battle with a vengeance. Ages of pent-up hatred came out against their larger, but outnumbered, foes. With the huge advantage of numbers, they began to have some success. The E3T members were spread out among them, partially to sway the battle and also to try to protect the Akara warriors during their first open battle.

Jocol became the spear point of the assault; he crashed into the enemy and carved open huge gaps in the skirmish line for the allies to exploit. Urghur fell at unprecedented rates as the superior numbers of the allied force, coupled with their deadly intent, turned the battle in their favor, and all of this without use of modern weapons to preserve ammo.

Victory in the end stunned the Akara, their first ever. They were agog with "first blood" and success in the new war against the Urghur. Although there were allied casualties, it seemed a minimal amount compared to what they thought would happen.

With the resounding win, now the Akara troops knew the enemy Urghur could be beaten.

Strewn all about, it was mostly Urghur bodies littering the clearing. Many had been killed at the hands of Jocol.

Brady had to literally grab Bralic to get his attention in his euphoria. "Bralic, focus. We can't sit here and celebrate. We need to drag the bodies out of sight in a hurry, and I'm sorry, but we can't take time to bury the dead Akara warriors. We're still in jeopardy in the open. Wake up."

"I'm sorry. Yes, you're right. Come, my brothers, we must act quickly now."

Shortly, they hurried back into concealing cover and resumed their trek, searching out the enemy.

Rosca walked up to Brady's side. "My warriors are pleased, Brady."

"That went better than I expected, but I suspect we were lucky. These Urghur soldiers fought poorly, for them. Still, it was a fight that could have gone either way."

Bralic added, "I think maybe they're not finding any of us to feed on, so they're becoming weakened."

"Possibly, but I wouldn't count on that. Perhaps there are isolated cases of that, but it may not be true everywhere. We approach every battle like they're at their peak."

"Yes, of course we should, Brady. I was just sharing our observations."

"I appreciate that, Bralic. Rosca, your folks have been fighting them all of your lives and for countless generations before that. I always want you to tell me your thoughts and observations."

"For us, it's new ground, standing up to them in battle and surviving. It was always sure death to fight, unless we could come upon occasional stragglers, but that was rare. They're normally very careful about what they do."

"If your Akara scholar is correct about the shared hive-mind idea, then they're all aware of this attack, and they'll make adjustments accordingly. As a matter of fact, I think I should contact all of my comrades to alert them of the newly increased danger."

After the call, he turned his head to Rosca as they walked along. "There were other fights, too, around the same time we had our battle. We didn't lose any of the battles, but just like us, there were people lost."

"That's a terrible consequence of war, but there is no other choice. It's time to press the Urghur troops because they've never been so vulnerable."

"I wish we had plenty of ammo to locate and assault their main bases. This level of fighting is going to be slow without modern weapons; it's tedious and incredibly dangerous."

"We know about sacrifice. Every one of my warriors is willing to do his duty if we can rid ourselves once and for all of these vermin. I hope your army can locate their home world and bomb them into oblivion. They're a curse upon all living things that needs to be eradicated."

"It's a nice thought, but I wouldn't bank on it. I have no idea where the fleet will go next."

"Rosca, you haven't really said much about Beca. What's your honest opinion about us training any of your females?"

"Although the council would have me think otherwise, as I've been around your women, I'm persuaded to give Beca her chance to follow her dream. If she can become such a magnificent creation as your women, it will be a matter of pride for all Akara. You do realize one of her main goals in this quest to remake herself is to draw your notice."

"I know that."

"Would you consider taking an Akara woman as your mate?"

"I seem to get that question a lot. I wouldn't let it get that far. Although I wouldn't trample her dreams, I'm not going to marry any woman from any race while I'm a soldier."

"I hear what you say, so help me to understand. Most of my warriors have mates, and yet we fight."

"When those warriors with mates are lost, they leave bereaved families behind, wives without a mate, children without a father."

"It is a tragedy, yet is that not true in your army too? I can't believe there are none who aren't married."

"We have married folk in our army, that's true. The E3T troops you see here are ones who've chosen to remain single. We let our married comrades be first in line to evacuate. With our personal choices, I'm not trying to say we're the only right way. It's just how we feel and how we approached it. Don't make us out to be noble martyrs. We're just grunts that drew the short straw by virtue of our choices."

"I'm not sure what that means, Brady, but we Akara don't agree with that premise. You are noble and worthy of our respect and esteem."

"Well . . . thanks for the respect and esteem, but that doesn't keep us all alive. We want to utilize our skills and experience to accomplish that for us and for you."

"I understand. We're learning many things from you, not only about your fine characters, but about battle tactics and tenacity in these fights. Perhaps Beca will succeed where you think she cannot."

Brady chuckled. "I very much doubt that. She'll make a great wife for somebody, someday."

Moving ahead, suddenly Bontag signaled by raising his fist. Everybody dropped down and slunk off the path into the concealing underbrush. A large column of Urghur came into view. They were greater in numbers than Brady felt able to engage in a fight, so they let them pass by. For the Akara, being this close to the enemy without dying was invigorating. Fresh off their first victory, already they were feeling a level of invincibility with the E3T members in their midst.

Brady was amazed the Urghur soldiers didn't sense his people, although he had no basis to judge their abilities, whatever they might be.

This sizeable enemy troop took some time to pass through before Brady could lead his unit out of hiding to continue their trek.

"They came from up ahead, so I'm going to assume they must have a base up there. I'd like to locate that base for future reference. As we accumulate enemy weapons and more of our people get modern arms, we might be in a position later to take it to them in their lair."

"I pray for that day," Rosca replied.

"I also," Bralic added.

"Well, that day will be a blood bath, so be careful what you wish for, my friends."

Rosca got a troubled look.

Continuing the patrol, they walked for another hour before finding their target. It was an amazing array, skillfully situated and constructed into the forest so the unwary would never see the danger and could wander into sure death. It was the skill of Bontag with his uncanny senses that halted them just short of betraying their presence to the hidden sentries guarding the base.

It was as Brady expected, a base teeming with enemy troops. Planet-wide they might be reduced, but there were plenty of them left to pose a terrible challenge. Victory was no sure thing, for a number of reasons.

Chapter Four

Carefully slinking away, Bontag led them in a different direction to exit the area. Using utmost caution, they managed to avoid detection. However, Brady had learned some important things about his foe. Seemingly, they had no abnormal special abilities, whether of smell or other ways, to detect allied troop presence. It was a very good development to learn the Urghur army was on a more even footing with the allied fighters than he'd thought. It was the idea of their single-hive-mind universal link and their ferocity in battle that was still the daunting challenge, in addition to the horror of their practices, like tearing apart and eating live captives.

Returning back up the mountain to the safety of the cave, Brady called again on his communication device to get reports from the other E3T units. Miraculously, every recon had been successful, with many having no battles at all.

Just as he concluded his talk, he turned his head to see Beca smiling.

"Hello, Brady, I'm glad you returned safely. I worried the whole time you were gone."

"Thank you, Beca, but remember, we're trained, experienced troops. That means we know what we're doing out in the field. Things can happen, but don't sit here imagining the worst when we're away. It will drive you crazy."

"I'm anxious to start my training. Is that acceptable to you?"

"Sure, I already said that. We'll see how you feel after a few days with the ladies."

"You think I will fail. I look forward to proving you wrong." She spoke determinedly, grimacing. Her eyes were full of challenge as she took his dismissive response as an affront.

Brady shrugged. "Okay, Beca. Good luck with that."

She eyed him coolly, misperceiving his tone and the skeptical look remaining on his face. "I've heard Misty and Sara say on many occasions how you make them want to slap the smirk off your face. Now I understand. You're a frustrating man."

Brady laughed. "I am that, guilty as charged."

"Is this how all human men are?"

"That would be true for some of us."

Glowering, she turned on her heel and departed stiffly. "I will leave you now. I have my business to attend to."

"Goodbye, Beca."

Looking back after a few steps, Beca paused and eyed him thoughtfully before continuing to walk away. She was clearly provoked, but to what extent and to what end, Brady could only guess. He chose to leave her training exclusively to the ladies and to avoid the area they'd set up for that training, as watching her pain wasn't something he cared to see. Knowing from personal experience what she'd be going through, Brady would do other things to avoid seeing it.

After briefly watching her walk away, Brady turned and went to take care of his own business. After the battle, there was a new war at hand, and they needed to carefully consider how they conducted it. Captured Urghur weapons were a boon, but they needed so many more before they could take meaningful actions. He hated wasting ammo training Akara warriors to shoot, but there was no way around it.

Brady increased his pace when he heard the distinct sound the enemy weapons made as he approached the impromptu firing range. Jocol and Bontag were busy overseeing the mass of eager Akara warriors trying to attain skills with modern weapons.

"Beca is off to start her training?" asked Rosca rhetorically.

"She is. This will be one tough day for her to endure."

"She knows that. Have some faith in her. She's driven to succeed, no matter how difficult the path."

"We need to capture more Urghur weapons, but equally important is stocking up on their ammo. Somehow we're going to need to raid one of their ammo caches."

"What did you have in mind?"

"Nothing yet. Bumbling around blindly, trying to stumble onto one isn't much of a plan. However, I have nothing better at this point."

"We may be of some help. Over time, we've noted the places they guard more heavily. I assume these must be the important places, like storage areas."

"That's logical. It would also mean they'd still have concentrated forces around those places, so it would be a serious battle. They'd be fully armed, and we'd still be at a disadvantage with too few of your warriors with modern arms. Your people are striving hard, but they're not at the level of marksmen yet. It's almost a no-win situation."

"We accept the risks of this approaching war. The time for sitting back, cowering in our holes, is over. If we must die to eradicate the Urghur scourge, we will do it gladly."

"I know that, Rosca. I don't question your bravery. I'm trying to be certain we win in the end so your surviving women and children aren't helpless before a victorious rampaging Urghur horde."

"A noisome thought indeed, my brother. As always, we defer to your wisdom and experience in war."

"We have experience, but not like this. Being in the corps is like having an umbrella over you all of the time. Now we have no superiority of weapons and no air cover. I'm in the dark as much as you at this point. I want you to share your thoughts and observations, even about the most miniscule things. It may save me making some critical error at a critical time."

"It's strange you put us on an equal footing with your people. To us, you're so far above us."

"I think you can see the fallacy of that illusion. We can bleed and die too."

"I want to say, after Beca's decision, there are other young females asking to train and join the fight, many females."

"That will be your choice, Rosca. We have no problem with female fighters, obviously. Maybe it would be a good thing so Beca won't go through this alone."

"You may be right. I will rethink my initial reluctance. We've always seen females in a certain light; gentle, lovely creatures to protect and cherish. A militant version of them is . . . I don't have a word for it."

"No problem, Rosca. We don't have a word for it either. Our female soldiers can definitely rattle your fillings."

Rosca chuckled. "I don't know what that means. Were you making a joke?"

"It's not important. Yeah, it was a joke of sorts. It's a way of saying they're just as competent as males as fighters."

"I understand. Your ladies evoke us."

"They evoke us too."

"Do you think Misty and Sara know they're adored by all the Akara warriors?"

"I expect they can see what's obvious. Why do you ask?"

"I think some brave young warrior will take the first step to woo them. After one starts, many others will join the pursuit. Will this annoy them? Would they start to kill off the Akara suitors?"

Brady laughed heartily. "Your young men are in no danger of being killed off. If the ladies get to the point where they've had enough, the young men will have no problem understanding it."

"We don't know your ways about mating."

"I don't expect there will be any mating with Sara or Misty."

"The young ones have their dreams about a human bride nonetheless."

Brady shrugged his shoulders. "All I could say to them is good luck with that."

Rosca looked puzzled. "So often, I can't understand what you say. Were you genuinely giving them your approval or making sport?"

"I don't ridicule anybody, Rosca. If one of them could bag Sara or Misty, I would be shocked. That's what I'm saying. Chasing our women is a steep climb."

"I suspect our young men know that."

"Moving along, I'm going to send out more recon teams to cover more ground. I'll go with you to observe these sites you said were heavily guarded. Maybe we'll get lucky."

"We're ready whenever you choose, Brady."

"Obviously, this will mean most of the small teams will be made up of only Akara warriors. Will that be a problem?"

"We've lived on this land since the beginning, and we're still here. My people know how to avoid the Urghur soldiers in the field."

"Good. We assemble in an hour and send out the squads."

"We'll be ready."

Leaving a little later, Rosca walked in the lead. Bontag wasn't in this unit, as Rosca knew where they were going. Following Rosca,

Brady continued to ponder the difficult dilemmas with no real solutions coming to mind. *Perhaps that's because there are no solutions.*

The trek was a sizeable one as they traveled down the mountain and proceeded through riskier regions with sparser cover. Moving slowly to use the utmost caution, they encountered two enemy patrols, but they were at a distance. They managed to avoid detection, and Rosca led them steadily toward their goal.

They stopped for a brief break to rest and have a quick meal, and Rosca whispered to Brady.

"It's been hazardous up to this point, but it will get worse from now on. I think we're near a major enemy stronghold, though I can't say for sure. We haven't actually seen it. This is much closer than we could have come before the war."

"I understand. It's why we came, so I've got no regrets."

"I hope we can avoid a major battle, but if it's meant to be, I'm ready."

"No goodbyes, Rosca. We're going to make certain there are no major battles until we're ready."

They forged forward cautiously, making slow time in trying to locate the Urghur base.

Suddenly, a large enemy patrol emerged from the forest, and they quickly dashed into a heavy overgrowth area. They waited in total silence until they passed.

"That was close," Brady whispered to Rosca.

"Yes."

The group decided to move through the difficult vegetation rather than go back into the open onto the trail, and to their surprise, they came upon an allied aircraft embedded in the undergrowth. They moved in close to inspect the wreck and discovered it wasn't a wreck.

Brady crawled up to look into the cockpit, which was undamaged. There was no blood or other sign the pilot was injured. With no body lying nearby, it was impossible to know what had happened to him or her.

"What do you think?" asked Rosca.

"I don't know."

Suddenly, the Akara warriors, who'd silently been searching the area, dashed into a bramble thicket. Brady heard a cry of shock and fear from a human voice. He rushed over in time to see the warriors pull the missing pilot from her hiding place. She was terrified, but when she saw Brady, she looked at him in shock.

The Akara troops released their hold on her.

"What is this?" she asked.

"Your rescue," Brady replied.

"Rescue?" She sounded out the word softly like it made no sense.

"You're not the only survivor down here, Captain. My name is Brady Black."

"Sonya Ashton. I thought I was dead. The enemy came to investigate my ship, but they didn't find me. These people you're with . . . are they . . ."

"They're the indigenous population, and now they're our allies. You're in no danger from them, ma'am."

"Please don't stand on formality. Call me Sonya."

"Okay. What's the status of your aircraft?"

"It got nicked up in the fight and knocked down here, but I think it will still fly, at least until it runs out of fuel, if I'm not careful about recharging."

"Is it still armed?"

"Sure."

"It would be good to have an air force again. I haven't seen any enemy aircraft since the end of the battle. I think the fleet carpet bombed everything enemy in sight. Their ground force numbers are greatly reduced."

"Thank God for that. I saw what they do to people. I thought that would be what happened to me. What are you doing out here?"

"We've started a plan to arm the native troops by taking Urghur weapons off their dead. Obviously, we need ammo, so we're looking for their bases to steal supplies."

"I understand."

"Do you think you can get that thing off the ground?"

"I can test a couple of things. Luckily, with this craft, I don't need a runway. I can ascend straight up."

"Well, let's get to it. I don't want to spend any more time in danger than is necessary."

"Sure, let's do this."

Crawling back into her cockpit for the first time since she'd crashed, Sonya ran some tests.

"The circuitry is fine; everything is responding as it should. I'm not going to test fire the engine, though. It would definitely draw enemy notice. I think it will fly, though."

"Good, do you want to stay here, or come with us to find the enemy base?"

"That's not necessary. If I take off, I'll have the view from the sky, and I can cover plenty of ground in a hurry. I just need somebody to point me in the right direction for where I land afterwards."

"Okay, Captain. Can you fit Rosca in with you? He can help spot any enemy camps and also point you to where we live in a mountain cave."

"That's fine, but landing on a mountainside, that's not going to work."

"We can land you at the base of the mountain and cover the craft with foliage. By the way, you're the only officer we know of on the planet. Technically, you're now in charge."

"I have no basis to lead army folk. I will exercise one officer privilege, though. I'm going to make a field promotion to make you a captain. I think you're in charge already anyway. I dub you Captain Brady Black."

Brady chuckled. "Gee, thanks, I don't know what to say."

"Don't say anything. As a field officer, you now have the same power to anoint other officers. We still need leaders."

"We do, no doubt about that. Rosca, are you up for flying in this fighter craft?"

"I . . . eh . . ."

"Good. Climb in. Captain, show Rosca where to sit."

She smiled at Rosca and his obvious fear. "Relax, we'll be just fine. It will be very cramped, but we'll make do. So, Brady, you're sure there are no more enemy vessels flying around?"

"We haven't seen any. That's the best I can tell you."

Sonya climbed in and then gestured to Rosca. He closed his eyes for a moment, steeling his courage before crawling into the cockpit with the allied pilot, the one-woman air force. His warriors eyed him anxiously, fearful for their chief.

"Good luck, Rosca. It was nice knowing you," Brady joked.

"Shut up, Brady," Sonya huffed. She closed the canopy and fired up the dual engines. In moments, there was a popping sound and tearing sound as the craft ripped out of the entangling caress of clinging vines, which tried to tie it to the ground. The roar of the engines echoed across the area and was certain to draw notice.

"We need to get out of here now!" Brady shouted over the roar of the engines.

The craft pivoted midair and edged forward. Immediately, Sonya opened fire on ground forces racing to investigate her sudden appearance. They attempted to return fire with their handheld weapons. It was a doomed strategy, and a great number of enemy troops were felled in a short amount of time.

Following her path of destruction, Brady's troop raced along, weaving through the numerous dead Urghur soldiers strewn all about, picking up enemy weapons as they went. Ahead, Sonya went into full attack mode on the ground forces of the enemy.

"That's got to be the base," Brady huffed as they sprinted along. "Come on, everybody."

Running along for about half an hour, they came to the site of Sonya's attack. The concealing forest and underground had been blasted back. Again, there were huge numbers of Urghur casualties. However, there were still enough live troops to pose a real threat for Brady's small recon force. A bitter battle quickly ensued. However, Brady still had an aircraft overhead to tip the scales in his favor. As with all others of the Urghur, none ever looked to surrender, so it was a fight to the death, down to the last soldier. This time, nearly all of the Akara warriors were firing Urghur weapons.

When it was done, Sonya landed near the front gate.

"Thank you for blasting these bastards into oblivion. I'm thinking we load some weapons and ammo into the aircraft to take back home. Is fuel a problem?"

"That is the least of our worries. As long as there is a sun, I can recharge indefinitely. Running out of ammo will be a problem, though. There's nothing at Urghur bases we can use in my aircraft weapons systems."

"Okay, but it's good if you can make numerous trips back and forth. We can solve a lot of problems by getting this much enemy ammo and weaponry back to our base camp."

"I'll take a few things this first time while I have a passenger. Once I know where to land, I can handle all of the subsequent trips flying alone. We can get this done in a hurry."

"We'll stand by here in the meantime. Hopefully, the enemy won't have any forces close enough to attack us while you're gone."

"By the way, my scopes still have picked up no sign of enemy air traffic."

"So far, so good."

"Thank you for finding me, Brady."

"You're welcome. Thank you for surviving in a hostile environment."

"I'll be back shortly."

"We'll be waiting."

With so few warriors, Brady couldn't really deploy a skirmish line. Instead, they waited in concealment, just in case. This fight had gone surprisingly well. Brady always anticipated adverse turns in fortunes. Here, they could afford no failures and setbacks. They had to be perfect every single time in whatever they did.

He still carried his E3T weapons, but never intended to use them. The thought crossed his mind, *We had weapons caches too. If we can find any that weren't destroyed in the bombing, we can reload and also arm the Akara with our weapons.*

That made him smile. It was a smile that didn't last long, however. They heard the sounds of enraged Urghur soldiers racing toward them.

Like it was a miracle, just as they emerged from the forest to attack Brady's little band, overhead, Sonya roared to their defense, annihilating the Urghur soldiers with the ease of a video game. There was little left for the Akara to do except mop up when Sonya was done decimating the enemy troop.

Sonya landed, and Brady raced over to her. "Thanks for saving our bacon again. By the way, I was thinking maybe we've got some weapons stored in various places that didn't get blasted by the bombing. We can reload our weapons, and maybe we find aircraft ordnance too."

"That would be fortuitous, to say the least. I can fly virtually anywhere on this planet. Maybe if I find possible pots of gold, we contact your units in those areas to come and help me. I can't place ordnance on this aircraft all by myself."

"Good. Our hopeless situation is getting brighter by the minute."

"I'll start with flying over my original base to see if there's anything left. Planet-buster weapons don't usually leave much behind that's salvageable."

"We can hope for the best. Actually, your onboard communication unit can contact any of our field radios better than mine. You could establish a stronger link than we can. Even when the aircraft is on the ground, we can run our periodic reporting sessions through you and have clearer reception by far."

"Okay, that's fine, Captain."

"I'll never get accustomed to that term."

"You will, Brady. It's how it needs to be now. We need to re-establish command and control to coordinate our efforts across this globe. You need to make your picks and field promote your choices right away. Somebody has to be in charge at each location."

"Sure, Sonya, I'll get right on it."

"Are you mocking me?" She eyed him quizzically.

"No, of course not." He smirked and then chuckled.

Sonya pondered him a moment before replying. "Oh, really? Because it sure sounded like it to me. Are you one of those guys that can't cope with females being in authority? Did you plague Mommy as a little nipper?"

Brady snickered. "Wow, you've got this whole scenario worked out in your mind. Ask my ladies about me. I have no problems with women in authority, or in any other role."

"You mean like warming your bed? I will ask them."

"Good, do it." Brady shook his head. "And 'no' to your snide comment about warming my bed. If a guy tries something like that with E3T women, they will feel the pain, if they survive at all."

"Good, my kind of women."

The two eyed each other for a moment with mirthful smiles.

"I think we're on the same side, Sonya."

She chuckled. "We are."

"So, are you going to let me live?"

"For the moment, but watch it, dude."

"You are a trip, ma'am."

"I am that, and I'm proud of it. Even in this day and age, women are always fighting their way uphill. Men are so stupid sometimes."

"Maybe I need to warn you; the Akara males are fascinated by our women, and that's probably too weak a word. You need to use your head about using this kind of display with them. They won't get it, and we don't need to put our alliance in jeopardy. They don't pose a problem, but they do ogle you a great deal."

"What was it you just said? I'll get right on it, Brady."

Brady shook his head again. "My God, what have I gotten into?"

"Well, enough of this fun. Back to work about your idea. I'm taking off to try to find ammo for you guys and for my aircraft."

"Let us know what you find."

"I will."

"Be careful out there."

"Always."

Brady watched Sonya's ship gracefully ascend skyward. They raced away and were quickly out of sight. Turning, he walked back toward the camp in the cave, making the best time he could while using necessary caution for Urghur threats.

It was nearly time for supper when he arrived. Beca's first training day was drawing to a close. Brady was curious, but he left it to the women to bring him an update or progress report.

A little later, when he was sitting down with food and drink, they found him. Beca was wobbly as she walked. Having exhausted muscles turn to rubber was a familiar feeling for Brady. Beca's initial training to build her muscles and core were difficult and vital. That needed to be accomplished before they could move on to hand-to-hand fighting, weapon's training, and battle tactics.

"Are you okay, Beca?"

"I'm fine," she muttered with little conviction.

Brady looked at Sara and Misty. Misty said, "She did great, Brady. This first stage, building up her muscles, is tough sledding."

"I hear that. I remember it well. Beca, you need to shovel plenty of food in your mouth to help your muscles grow."

"I'll get a plate for you," said Sara.

Beca, totally spent, collapsed beside Brady.

"We tried to warn you," Brady explained.

"Shut up, Brady," said Misty. "She knows all of that. We've got this."

"Sorry." He shrugged his shoulders and gave a meek smile.

When Sara returned, Beca gobbled down the food and then looked at Sara. She smiled. "I'll get another plate for you."

"Thank you," Beca said with a rasp.

"You're doing great, honey," Misty whispered. "The first week is the worst. After that, you start to make gains and the pain and soreness lessen."

"I hope so."

"Trust me; we've all been through it. By the way, you're going to have a head start on your friends. We've got a large number of young Akara gals that want to join you in training."

"Really?"

"Really. They'll start tomorrow so they can be at the same stage with you. You'll be surprised how fast all of you become competent fighters."

"That will be a great day. Although, I'm sure it doesn't make the men happy."

"Don't worry about the men. We don't."

They all looked at Brady.

"Don't start, ladies. I already got an earful from Sonya earlier today. Give me a break, please."

"Whatever," Misty replied dismissively.

"On that happy note, I'll leave you to your ruminations. *Vaya con dios, señoritas.*"

"Go with God? I didn't know you knew Spanish."

"Bits and pieces. That's true of quite a few languages. I'm secretly a scholar."

The ladies all laughed, including Beca.

"I like this," she said. "What's your word? Rapport?"

"Yeah, Beca, you have rapport with a jarhead. That's hardly something notable."

"Hey, I object! Speak for yourself," Sara interjected. "Getting attuned with Misty and me is notable. You should have said 'male jarhead,' because we're not subject to your same shortcomings. You're the ones with those faulty XY chromosomes."

"Right, ladies. By the way, you are delusional."

Chapter Five

True to the prediction, after the first week of training, the young Akara women recruits felt better, and uniformly they were getting stronger. The improvement greatly motivated them in their goals, and from that point forward, they made steady progress. The reaction in the Akara community was one of surprise and of a level of pride as their young women transformed toward their new physical standard, the human women soldiers.

Toning their bodies had the predictable effect; it drew the intense notice of the males. Where normally at this age these girls considered the romantic advances of the males with marital bonding in mind, instead, these girls were driven in their goals and dismissed those clumsy male advances, making them irresistible in the minds of the young men.

It caused an additional, unexpected request. Brady was asked to institute similar training for the Akara males, as if this would raise their worthiness in the eyes of their own females. The rampant, adolescent fantasies were mildly amusing, though taking time away from the war effort wasn't practical.

"The best we can do is to sprinkle in some training and to give various exercises for them to do on their own," Brady explained to Rosca.

"That's good enough," Rosca replied. "I think our male warriors are not in need of much training. We're already good fighters."

"I agree, based on what little I've seen out in the field. I understand what they want. I really do, but if the Urghur soldiers find us here and come in numbers, we need all of our troops at full readiness."

"Of course, that's my point exactly. Although increasing their skills with new tactics, and also strengthening them, would seem to me to be a good idea."

"You really would like the young men to train?" Brady muttered thoughtfully. He looked away while he pondered the supposition and the ramifications.

"They would be better fighters. Our old ways centered on hunting for food and eluding the enemy. That doesn't make us competent in warring against the Urghur horde. Prior to your coming, it was sufficient, but I can see how we should have done things differently."

"Don't second guess your past. With the severe discrepancies of your primitive arms versus their modern arms, their hive mentality, and brutal natures, it was a no-win situation. We look ahead rather than behind, agreed?"

"Nonetheless, I'm the chieftain. I have the responsibility for the safety of my people. I need to review what I do and find better ways to proceed."

"Okay, that's fine. From my point of view, you did pretty well. You could have been totally wiped out as a people by the swarm. You're still standing here, and that speaks volumes."

"It's a small consolation, with how many lives have been lost over so long a time. As your ladies said earlier, there were so many good people lost, friends from forever. Those were terrible, wasted deaths that served no purpose; our friends and family members were reduced to food for those worthless, savage beasts. It's appalling."

"It is. However, dwelling on it will drive you crazy, because we can't bring any of them back. Lock onto the mission that's ahead of us. Now the only thing we can do is save the current people for a better future."

They sat together in thought for a moment longer before Brady asked, "We've surmised they're like a hive and a swarm, and that means they must have a queen somewhere birthing their young. Let me ask you, have you ever seen any Urghur young?"

"No."

"That would mean possibly that they import their troops from elsewhere, like a home world. If the supply line of prisoners being sent off-world was interdicted, it might mean the supply line of replacement troops coming here ended also, which would mean we have a shot at killing them off. Each kill we make anywhere on the globe is one less we will ever have to face again. This is just speculation on my part. There are certainly other theories."

"I feel you're right in this opinion. We've seen nothing to the contrary, and the battles we've had now are different than fighting them in the past."

"I think you might have a point that they're less successful in feeding now, and it's weakening them."

Brady's radio chirped to life. He listened as Sonya directed troops elsewhere to meet her at a distant allied base.

"My flyover makes me think this base was missed in the bombing. I think we might have hit a mother lode of supplies."

Brady smiled.

"This is a good thing," Rosca muttered.

"This is a very good thing."

Continuing to monitor the chatter coming over the radio, the good news got better when she landed and met her E3T ground troops. Not only did they find an intact base with vital supplies, food, weapons, and ammo, they found other E3T troops, base personnel, and intact aircraft and pilots. It was an incredible boon, and it changed a tenuous battle situation into a clear advantage for fighting the remaining Urghur.

Brady listened as Sonya talked to the base commander. Colonel Staka Severn, a nonhuman officer, explained, "At the end, our fight with the horde was in close quarters, so there was no way to evacuate us. I'm not sure why the fleet just up and left. All that we knew was we were marooned and had to fend for ourselves. The enemy just pulled out suddenly, and though we've spotted their patrols in numbers, they've kept their distance. We're well supplied because this was a transit point for troops being deployed across the entire area."

"I can't tell you how happy we are to find you. We've established a relationship and an alliance with the indigenous people and have been fighting the Urghurs ever since."

"Urghurs? That's their name?"

"Listen, obviously you're the new commander in this theatre, as we haven't found any surviving officers elsewhere yet. I made a field promotion of Brady Black to captain."

"I know of Brady, by reputation. He's a good man."

"I think we should bring all of the other field-promoted people here to meet and make a plan. Now that I'm not alone up in the air, we can transport people and materials in a hurry and locate the Urghur strongholds."

"Agreed."

Brady looked at Rosca. "I guess I'm in for a road trip. Since that base is intact, my guess would be they have more than just the fighters. They probably have transport craft too. I'm going to take you with me to that meeting. We've got people here to leave in charge."

"If you think that is wise."

"Somebody needs to represent the interests of the Akara, and who better than you?"

Rosca shrugged his shoulders. "I will go tell my people about this."

"Okay, I'll talk with you later. I need to tell my unit about this good news."

When Brady walked off to find his troops, he found Bontag and Jocol had started informal training with the avid young Akara warriors. Bralic was there, along with a considerable number of the older warriors too. They were ostensibly to be observers, but most of them had started the exercises too.

"Hey, Bralic."

"Brady."

"Bontag, Jocol, come here a moment. Listen, Sonya found an intact base across the planet from here. We now have a living bird colonel to take command, and we've got other E3T troops, squadrons of fighter craft and the pilots, and plenty of supplies. I'm taking Rosca with me to the base for a sit-down. Bralic, you'll be in charge back here until we get back, okay?"

Bralic smiled.

"Don't let it go to your head, dude."

Bralic laughed. "I don't know what you mean."

"Sure you don't."

They all laughed.

"How's this going with the warriors, Bralic?"

"They're driven. It's going well. What our women are doing has really resonated, and they want to get in front of this new normal. I've even gotten requests from some to join your corps."

"What did you tell them?"

"I didn't say yes or no. I just said, 'Show us what you've got.'"

"Good answer. We should be back before too long. With these new aircraft in play, we should be able to sweep the planet and tag the enemy camps fairly rapidly. If there are any remaining enemy aircraft, we can take them out."

Brady had no more than walked away from his friends when they heard the roar of a large transport craft landing at the impromptu landing site at the base of the mountain. Brady hurried down the mountainside along with Rosca. Sonya had accompanied the transport vessel in her fighter.

She approached Brady. "I'm fueled up, loaded up, and fired up to get this party started."

Brady laughed. "Good job, ma'am. I've decided to take Rosca along, so the colonel gets off on the right foot with our allies."

"No problem. Load him in and let's go."

Rosca was nervous as he took a seat. "Buckle in," Brady explained as he took a seat beside Rosca.

The flight around the globe floored Rosca as he saw his world from the sky for the first time.

The transport stopped at other settlements to pick up more people. Brady saw many others of his original hundred survivors in happy E3T reunions.

Once they landed at the base, it was strange to be back on a fully functioning E3T facility. Those troops Brady had field-promoted to officer status, the colonel came out to meet. He surprised them all by immediately supplying captain uniforms and insignia.

"Welcome to the officer corps," said the colonel. "I'm Staka Severn, in case some of you don't know me."

"We all know you, sir," said Brady.

"This is Air Corps Major Walter Whalen, my second-in-command, and also the officer in charge of the air wings."

"I'd like to introduce Rosca, chieftain of his tribe of the Akara, our allies in the war against the Urghurs."

"Hello, it's my honor to be here on behalf of my Akara people."

"Hello, Rosca. Welcome to the base. We're happy to have you."

"It's very impressive." Rosca glanced around at the facilities and equipment in admiration as they walked.

"Colonel, they were kind enough to give us shelter and food right after the evacuation when we were stranded. More importantly, they extended their trust. We've fought shoulder to shoulder since that time in beating back the Urghur troops we've faced. I'm proud to call them friends."

The colonel pondered the explanation briefly before replying. "Okay, Brady. We'll accept your opinions and observations. We need all of the help we can get at this point."

"Do you still have a communication link with the fleet?"

The colonel looked at the major before answering. "Brady, at this point, assume we're on our own. Whether that will change in the future, we'll see."

"Since you didn't answer the question, I gather there's more to the story."

"I guess there's no reason to dance around the truth. Walter and I have talked about that last battle and what happened afterwards. There was just no precedent we could think of to explain how it was handled, or mishandled. Our speculation is somebody in charge made a command decision back home as the battle went south. They pulled the plug and called back our forces."

"By that, you mean pulled the plug prematurely."

"That is a distinct possibility. We all speculate on these wars we're thrown into as to who makes the calls. It's possible somebody who is paid to do the prelims knew what to expect here and sent us anyway. Once we started to get hammered, they pulled out under the pretext of another pressing engagement. Since we've sent messages and gotten no response, our guess is nobody back home wants to take responsibility, or even to acknowledge what happened here. Keeping it from coming to light surely means pretending we all got dusted off."

"Wow. I have no words for that."

"This is why we were hesitant with Rosca, Brady. It wasn't any concerns about him. It was having him see the truth about us."

Brady looked at Rosca, who was clearly taken aback, but quickly composed himself before speaking to the new E3T allies.

"My new friends, the Akara people can be trusted to be your partners in any war. I think Brady can attest to that. What you've said about what happened among your people is very distressing and sad. That you could be abandoned by your own leaders is troubling. We have no precedent for such a thing"

"Distressing indeed, it is that."

"We don't have . . ."

"Poor behaviors like that?" Brady replied. "I tried to tell you not to idolize us. We're not better people than you."

"If this is your fate, to live here among us, it isn't a problem."

Brady looked at the two officers in charge. Colonel Severn answered. "I appreciate your offer, and we have no problem living among you. However, please understand we will endeavor to eventually return to our own homes, in spite of the complications back there."

"That's understandable. Whatever accommodations you need, we will provide as we are able. We owe you so much for your help against the Urghur menace. From what you've said, it would seem some among your chiefs would have reason to plot that your return might be unwelcome."

"That's why we're handling this very carefully. If we managed to call back the fleet, it might not go well for us or for the Akara."

"They would attack us? Why?"

"I'm just letting you know what you might be dealing with."

Rosca looked at Brady.

"Don't bother wasting your breath," he replied. "We already know what a predicament we may have caused for you and your people. What I can tell you is that we will stand with the Akara against all foes, Urghurs or otherwise."

"You would fight your own people?"

"I think you can see it may be a fight we wouldn't want, but one that could be forced on us. There are unworthy people with power back home."

"That also is very distressing."

Brady looked at the colonel and the major. "Do you have a guess about who the culprit might be?"

Colonel Severn replied, "It would need to be someone at or near the top, but also someone with ties back at headquarters. I don't think it would be the force commander. I would suspect one of the top advisors, like the representative from the intelligence service, or maybe the rep from the corporate sponsors. It's no secret they supply a flood of money to gain influence in high places."

"That would be my guess too."

"The culprit, or culprits, would have motives, like profiting from these invasions. We've all talked about the possibility of impure motives in the orders that come our way. It's not beyond the realm of possibility that money is changing hands among the elite as they buy off power and influence."

"That makes me mad."

"Brady, it makes all of us mad."

"We're going to take care of the swarm and wipe out the vermin Urghurs. After that, we will see what we will see."

"Well, enough of the casual chat. Let's have this meeting with all of the reps and make a plan."

"Yes, sir."

The colonel opted to share their thoughts with all those gathered. Predictably, there was a room full of angry faces.

Cole Whitten, an experienced soldier Brady knew well, was sitting beside him. He muttered loudly, "Those damn bastards.

I thought the Urghurs were low, but our own people hanging us out to dry? Somebody is going to pay for this."

There was a universal response from everybody else, echoing the sentiment.

The colonel replied, "Let's keep it together, folks. Remember, you are officers now. You go back to your units and lead them. We have one primary mission, and that is taking it to the Urghurs. If you don't win there, nothing else matters anyway."

"Trust me, we will defeat the Urghur threat," Cole responded.

"Brady, do you want to explain what you told us earlier?"

Brady said, "Actually, I should have Rosca speak." He looked at Rosca who motioned for Brady to continue. "One of his people in another camp is a great brain and has studied the enemy long term. We've concluded they're like a colony of intelligent insects, like ants or bees, only they seem to share a single hive mind. What one experiences, they all experience. That's how they were always a step ahead of us. We think that they've lost their portal back to their home world, so they can no longer send captives there as food or send replacements and reinforcements here. As we kill them off, it's a steady decline in their forces, and they're weakening without adequate feeding. Each day that goes by, we're stronger and they're weaker. Rosca, do you have anything you'd like to add?"

"No, Brady, you've explained it well."

"Going on the assumption they have a queen who is located elsewhere, there is no other way to replenish after their losses. They're ripe for E3T justice."

"Boo-ya!" Even the colonel and major joined the martial shout.

The major spoke. "I'm sending our aircraft across the globe. We should be able to locate them in their hiding places and then take swift actions. We've got plenty of aircraft ordnance to cripple whatever is left of them. Stay tuned, folks."

The remainder of the conference included discussions about logistical matters as well as preliminary strategy ideas. There was uniform agreement that Visule should be elevated to an Akara leadership role, as well as counseling the combined leadership with his thoughts and observations.

The flight back home went swiftly. Walking back up the mountain, Brady saw Akara sentries were stationed outside, instead of doing it the old way of hiding inside the cave. They'd taken up nearly all of the practices of E3T, like salutes, ranks, and so forth.

Walking down the tunnel to the city, Rosca and Brady chatted and pondered a number of things. It happened that they passed the area where Misty and Sara were training the females, which at this point numbered in the thousands.

The females turned their heads to look *en masse* at the two men of importance. Rosca was their chief, and Brady was their heartthrob.

Beca shouted at him provocatively, "Hello, Captain Brady Black." She smirked, proud of her improved conditioning, and her increased confidence. "Would you like to teach us anything?"

He paused a moment at her loaded question. "Hello, Beca. I'll pass on the lessons. Misty and Sara are the perfect instructors for you."

"Soon we will be warriors. What do you say about that?"

"Ask me when you are warriors."

All of the young females laughed. They too savored the new experience of banter with an appealing male.

Brady walked away. Rosca was smiling.

"What?"

"I didn't expect this in our girls. They've far exceeded what I thought they would do. Perhaps they will become like your women."

"The rub comes later, if they get plugged into combat units. It's in our male natures that we protect any females. It can cause trouble in battles, because if a female goes down, men tend to collect around to protect her. It can cause weaknesses in the defense array. Do you see what I'm saying?"

"Yes. That is a difficult proposition. It's something to think about."

"Back on our home planet, Earth, long ago, the first army to add women into battle units noticed this phenomenon in the first fights. We've been trying to cope with it ever since. You can tell men 'don't do it,' but as I said, it's in our natures and we do it anyway."

"I can see that. I would do the same thing."

"One other aspect to this situation is the parents. I think Sala is happy with how things are going, but Bren is on the other side of the fence. I think he'd like to slug me."

Rosca chuckled. "I'm sure you're wrong about that. Bren respects you a great deal; we all do."

"We're talking about his daughter here. Daddies get very defensive about daughters. That's in our nature too."

Rosca shrugged his shoulders. "I can't say you're wrong. Females are our real treasure."

"My point exactly. I didn't come up with this idea of training your females. I didn't agree to it or support it, yet I get the blame."

"You're seen by us as the leader of your people, regardless of that colonel."

"That's an aspect in my life I've never had before, where I become responsible for the decisions and actions of others. I prefer being responsible only for me."

"I can't say I enjoy being the chief, but it became my charge. I do it for my people, not for any desires of my own. Do you see the difference?"

"Sure."

"I think you're stubborn in your ways. You know what I'm saying, but you don't want to concede that this applies to you. Real life isn't what we want it to be. Instead, it's independent of our desires, and it's not always fair. We do what we must."

"I feel so much better now that you clarified that."

Rosca laughed. "This is exactly what I was saying. Be obstinate if you wish, but in the end our duties catch up to us."

"That's true, but it doesn't mean I have to like it."

Rosca shook his head. "There's really nothing I can say to this."

"Now you've got it, my friend."

Meanwhile, Misty and Sara led their class out of the cave for training outside in the forest.

They trooped past Brady and Rosca, smiling as they went.

"Have fun, ladies," said Brady.

"We will," Misty replied. "Maybe everybody should stay in the cave for safety's sake. We're going to have weapons proficiency training with the primitive weapons out there. We don't want any accidents, with arrows flying all over the place and clueless men in the wrong place at the wrong time."

Brady chuckled. "Right, Misty. Thanks for the warning. I'll pass that on to the guards."

The young women nodded as they walked past. Every one of them smiled, filled with pride at their new outlook and status. They were the first, the vanguard of the future Akara female warriors.

Once they exited the cave mouth, Brady walked out with Rosca to watch them.

"It still amazes me, with this steep angle on the mountain, how sure the footing is with your little cleats for your people and for mine."

"With the marvels you've brought with your technology, it's nice we have something to offer too."

"At the top of that list of nice things, your decency as a people, trust, companionship, taking in strangers, you're a noble people, and we of the corps thank you."

"That's kind of you to say that."

"It's not just words, it's the truth. We wouldn't be alive now without help from you."

They looked up at the roar of ships landing. A large transport ship was accompanied by a fighter squadron of four.

"Wow, I wonder what this is about?"

They waited as the new arrivals made their way up the mountainside. Brady was surprised to see both the colonel and the major, a troop of their guards, and some Akara officials.

"Do you know them, Rosca?"

He looked stunned. "Only by reputation. The Akara scholar who we've spoken of is one of them."

The visitors approached, cautiously picking their steps on the treacherous pathway. Brady saluted the ranking officers.

"Welcome, folks."

Rosca spoke. "Brady, this is Visule."

"Greetings, Brady. I've heard a great deal about you."

"I hope that's good, sir."

Brady was surprised. Visule wasn't an ancient, studious-looking person. Rather, he was young and vital, and he looked like a competent warrior, with a muscular, physical stature and serious demeanor. As they walked, Brady noticed every female eyeing Visule, including the corps women. Visule made an impression, though he totally ignored the female glances.

"I know I look differently than what you expected," Visule related after a moment of perusal. "I hear that quite a lot."

"Your people have great respect for you, and you've earned a lot of celebrity among the corps. Your observations and insights about the Urghurs have given us an edge in fighting them; I'd say the key edge to the possibility of turning the corner in the upcoming war."

"Thank you, but let's not overvalue my research quite yet."

"Is something wrong?"

He looked at the colonel, who spoke. "Brady, is there someplace we can go to talk?"

"Sure, come inside the cave to the city. Hi, Sonya, it's nice to see you again."

"Hello, Brady. It kind of feels like I'm coming home, since this was my first abode on this planet. I was so lucky you found me, because my food and water were almost gone back then."

"We were lucky, too, in that the Akara didn't choose to fight us when we first met them."

Rosca replied. "Something in what you said and did made me think we could trust you, Brady. How you acted after dealing with the Urghur, it wasn't what we expected. We needed a break, as you would say, so I took a chance."

"You're very discerning, Rosca," Visule added. "If I have notoriety, I don't think you realize that you're also famous among the Akara everywhere. If there was such a position as high chief of all Akara peoples, you would be it."

"Me? That can't be."

"It can be, and it is."

Chapter Six

The file of dignitaries made their way along the tunnel, into the city, and then to the council sacred building.

"With your permission, I wish to include our council in this deliberation," Rosca said.

"That's understandable," Visule answered. "Is that acceptable, my friends?"

The colonel looked at Brady, who replied, "They're good people, sir."

"Okay, then lead the way."

When the group entered the holy chamber, the council members eyed them in curiosity. Rosca went over to explain to the head of the council. It was a first for any but designated Akara to enter the enclosure.

"You all know of Visule. He has come to us to share his thoughts. Will you listen?"

"We will, Chieftain. You are welcome here. Hello, Brady," the head of the council replied.

"Hello, gentlemen, thank you for allowing us into your sacred sanctuary. This is Colonel Staka Severn, the ranking officer of the corps on this planet, and this is Major Walter Whalen, the ranking officer of the air force. You already know pilot Captain Sonya Ashton."

"You're welcome also, friends. Please take seats and let us discuss this matter."

Taking seats meant sitting down cross-legged in a semicircle, as there were no chairs.

Also included in the visitor group for deliberations were senior Akara leaders from other camps. A total of twenty individuals had come to talk with the council in Rosca's community. Visule immediately addressed the group.

"I've come to discuss this war with the enemy Urghurs. We're all pleased that the fight has gone well thus far. However, I want to share with you another of my thoughts on the matter. I believe we're in danger of some complacency with what has been a series of seemingly easy victories. We've made assumptions about them, their combat readiness, and their numbers, which may not be accurate. Because the prior air attack of our new friends caused such great damage to them, we've concluded they're on the verge of defeat and collapse. It's a wonderful proposition, but I don't think it's true. My assessment is that the remaining core of their forces on this planet have retreated to a place or places of safety and concealment, much as we've done since they first came. I suspect there is a far greater threat than we hope for. Do you understand?"

"We haven't been able to detect those enemy concentrations with our scans," said the major.

"I would like to point out, you never detected us either," said Visule. "Once people go underground here, it seems to negate your detection devices."

"That shouldn't be possible, but perhaps he's right. Perhaps something in the nature of this planet does that very thing. If so, we're potentially skating on thin ice. It may be that not only do they still have formidable ground forces, they may still have hidden aircraft."

"That's a chilling thought, Colonel," said Brady. "I believe you're right about our thinking, Visule. We all thought perhaps we've turned the corner against the Urghurs. I guess a more accurate way to say it is 'hoped.'"

"I wish it were the case, but I don't think so. They're a society bred for war, but also bred to adapt to succeed every single time. They wouldn't go quietly, to use your terms."

"Have we been able to find other E3T survivors around this globe?"

"We have, but in small numbers thus far. We're certainly not going to be the daunting military force we were before when we got whipped. I doubt we'll end up fielding any more than a thousand of us. I hope I'm wrong about that."

The assemblage pondered the assessment grimly.

"The combined peoples of the Akara will stand with you. With your modern arms, perhaps we can defeat these Urghur savages."

"That's our hope, but we need to deal with this very carefully. If we uncover a site where they have overwhelming numbers in hiding, they could do some real damage before we can react to the threat. Our air corps is very limited. If they have fighter craft that suddenly emerge, it will be dicey at best at that point."

"Visule, I get the feeling there is more you have to say," Brady added.

"Well, I've given you my best guess about the probabilities we face. There is one other aspect, which is total speculation on my part. If my hive mentality and socialization model is true, I don't think they'd leave pockets of their . . . well . . . beings isolated from a queen like this. What I worry is that they have a replacement, perhaps a maturing young female pushed into becoming the new queen of this swarm. If she's hidden here somewhere, she may already be birthing new members for the swarm. I hope I'm wrong."

"That would be a game changer. I don't know their gestation period to mature the hatchlings, but it may be quicker than we can adjust to. Ultimately, even with the intact E3T base, we still have a finite amount of ammo and supplies. For food, we can feed off the planet, but we have no way to replace spent ammo for a protracted war."

"Hence, the reason for our visit," said the colonel.

"Wow, the bad news never ends," Brady muttered.

"We have faith in you," said Rosca.

Brady didn't bother responding.

The council members' normally serene expressions faded as the import of the revelation sunk in. For them, going back into the mode of "dodge and survive" that had been their lives for countless generations, having the feelings of hope snatched away was more than they could emotionally tolerate at that moment.

Brady felt helpless, like it was his personal flaw that he had no ready answer to solve the problem. It was depressing for him that, once again, the imminent possibility of his demise was back on the table; however, he felt badly for the Akara too. They'd endured so much for so long a time that having their hope snatched away was cruel.

"Damn it," he muttered.

Brady looked at the resident genius in the room, Visule, and he appeared to be equally at a loss. Noticing Brady's glance, Visule responded apologetically, "I'm sorry, but I have no plan to recommend about this. Matters of war tactics and strategies are out of my realm. The warriors must make the best choice from their knowledge and experience base, and then we must do our utmost to survive."

"No one is expecting miracles from you, Visule. The fact you could warn us out of our false illusions is huge. At least now we can try to properly prepare and not be suddenly surprised by the enemy. We make best use of the remaining ordnance we have to take out as many of those things as possible."

Brady looked at the colonel.

"You don't need me signing off on your statement, Brady. We all acknowledge the obvious, and of course, under these circumstances, we cope."

"If we could find where they keep the queen, that would give us the chance to bomb the nest and maybe kill her off. Obviously, that would involve getting lucky in finding them and not setting off an overwhelming response from the Urghur troops before we could strike."

The colonel added, "By the way, Brady, I've ordered all of our troops to train with Akara weapons, so if we exhaust the ammo supply, we have skill with the remaining primitive weapons from here on this planet."

"Good idea, sir. My little crew here did that already."

"How's your project going with training the female Akara fighters?"

"It's in the early stages, but the young ladies are doing well, from what I've been told."

"That idea has been floated in the other settlements, and I expect there will be more volunteers to join their men in the fight in the future."

Brady looked at Rosca and the council members. None said anything, but the concern on their faces spoke volumes.

"I'm sorry. I know this is a shock, and it seems we're ruining your society."

Rosca responded. "No, Brady, it's not what you think. Of course we long for the old ways, but we've accepted things must change for us to survive. The disturbing thought is our young Akara females, while trying to be warriors, get caught up in the jaws of those monsters and are ripped apart and consumed alive. It haunts us."

"It haunts us too. I have those same fears about our ladies, Misty and Sara."

"We must find that queen, because the key to victory would seem to be there. If we fail, I think perhaps these Urghurs will finally wipe us out in the end."

"We will find a way," said Brady impulsively. He had absolutely nothing to back up his proposition, but emotionally he felt the need. It bolstered the spirits of everybody. Even the aged council members got fire in their eyes.

"I've never been somebody to give up, no matter what."

"Thank you, Brady," Rosca replied. "We will not go quietly either."

"Visule, can you suggest anything in regards to Urghur behavior to guide us? Is there anything they do that might tip us off as to where to look?"

"That's a difficult request. Their forces would be concentrated around protecting the queen above all else, but those forces would mostly be hidden, whether underground or in some other place of seclusion. With that being said, in the vicinity of the entrance, they would deploy considerable defensive forces, more so than anyplace else we find. Does that help?"

"It's a start. Our issue is stumbling into that place. Not only could we be overwhelmed in a hurry, we'd also tip them off that we'd found the queen. That could spur them to release the next version of their swarm attack."

Rosca interjected. "If we found that main nest, the entire of the Akara people would mass together to fight that key battle. Although it would leave the settlements vulnerable, it seems the best choice is to win or lose in a final decisive battle."

"That's definitely rolling the dice, Rosca. Trying to move troops gathered together from all over the planet would take time. We need to think about that plan to see if there's a better idea before we go with an all-or-nothing scenario. I don't like to lose. If we lose, the innocents pay the ultimate price."

"What I can't tell you is the result of that battle," Visule added. "If we were to be so fortunate as to kill the queen, what would be their behavior? I don't know. It would be nice to imagine they'd lose heart and would die off or become easy targets at that point. However, the more probable possibility is they'd be thrown into a suicidal rage and we would be forced to kill every single one of them to finally be free of the threat. That would mean considerable casualties for our people. I'm sure of it."

"If this immature queen hastened maturing, and if she's been cranking out young at record rates, we could be in for a fight with no certainty of the outcome."

"That is very true, Brady."

"My unscientific opinion is that the Urghurs won't go off and abandon this planet without some means to replenish their ranks. If they severed the link here, it may have been because of our appearance and the war, but I suspect it just may be that they turned to another world or worlds to conquer and exploit. They could come back here at any time. This would still be an easy food source, from their point of view. That's a big incentive for a voracious species that can never seem to get enough to eat."

"I hope we can uncover more ammo caches," the colonel interjected. "However, for purposes of our planning, we must assume what we have is what we're going to have to work with."

"I agree, sir."

Rosca spoke. "We've been successful in accumulating Urghur weapons and their ammo. We're much better off than at any time in our history. Now we can go into battles on a much stronger footing. My people have learned what you taught them about modern warfare; we're skillful in killing Urghurs, and in finding more of their hiding places. It was never safe for us to look before in our weakness."

"That's a good thing," Brady muttered. "Of course, it helped that the fleet bombed the hell out of them before they left."

"What do you say about Beca and her class of trainees?"

"They're coming along nicely. Obviously, they're not at a point to go in the field yet, but their progress is very good. Not only are they learning to fight, but the strengthening exercises are having speedy affects toning them up. Misty and Sara have been complimentary, and that is high praise coming from them. They don't give out idle compliments."

"I can truly say, we men of the Akara people are proud of those girls. It's a good development in our society. Honestly, I doubted they would stick to it, but they've surprised me."

"Giving up the old way of looking at females from your perspective, I understand how difficult it is from your background. We've had our women as our equals for a very long time, so for us, we're not surprised at the progress."

"They're still young ladies with their heads full of ideas, Brady. Do you understand that?"

He smiled. "I'm flattered; however, we've got work to do."

"Yes, we do. For us, the idea of those girls going into battle against the Urghurs is still very distressing."

"The better way to look at it is having those girls being able to defend themselves. It's imminently better than the alternative of being easy meat."

"We haven't been people that faced change often in our history. It's an adjustment."

"Understandable. Listen, I've got something to take care of. I'll talk to you later, Rosca."

"Goodbye, Brady."

Brady walked away, heading to the joint hut that was the new home of the five E3T members, he picked up some equipment he needed for a planned foray outside. When he walked back out of the hut, ironically he ran into Beca, who was on her way to her family hut. Brady didn't see her on a daily basis like he had when he was living with her host family.

"Beca."

"Hello, Brady." Her smile was like a smirk with her new confidence. The strengthening exercises done over the long term had sculpted her body to its best possible state. Taut, supple, and curvaceous, she was on par with Missy and Sara now. Definitely eye-catching, she basked in the awed admiration of the males around her. It was unprecedented for Akara females.

They stared at each other a moment.

"Did you have a question?" she asked, smiling smugly.

He chuckled. "I did not. It's good to see you. I gather you're at a good place in your training."

"I think we've completed all of the early phases. Our bodies have become like our human friends. We're ready for more, wouldn't you say?"

"You look very nice, Beca."

"We've wondered why you men don't step in now to add to our training. I'm not saying we lack for anything having Misty and Sara guiding us, but perhaps you could add a new dimension. That is, unless you fear to face us." She smirked again.

"You've got me there. I am terrified to face a pack of rabid Akara women warriors."

They both laughed.

"Brady, I look forward to the day when you can see me with different eyes. I'm not a little girl any longer."

"I know that."

"Well . . ."

"I'm not sure what you want for me to say at this point. I've explained how it is in the corps."

"Yes, we've asked Misty and Sara about that. They say there are many married soldiers in your corps."

"With the Urghur problem, my focus has to be there."

She eyed him thoughtfully. "Okay, as you wish."

Turning, she walked away. She was an impressive sight, capable of stirring him, just like Misty and Sara.

Brady turned and left to find his handpicked unit for the day. They were already gathered and waiting for him. Soon, they departed the cave, headed down the mountainside, and past the landing pad. Traveling away in a different direction, they moved swiftly, as they had a long distance to cover and were going into new territory.

On this day, the mix of his troops came from the finest of the Akara, young males who were skilled, talented, and fearless compared to their older counterparts. They were perfect for Brady's purposes. Just like with Beca and her training, these troops were part of the future, the new wave of the Akara military. The old fears, prejudices, and reluctance were gradually being weaned away. These Akara no longer harbored feelings of inevitable loss when facing the Urghurs. They'd seen enough different results in their actual fights to reinforce their confidence.

Just like the females, with time these young Akara had also done extensive strength and agility training and had re-sculpted their bodies. Combined with their natural assets of tracking, stealth, and knowledge of the Urghurs, they were a lethal force if they came upon enemy soldiers. Every one of them carried modern arms, whether E3T weapons or captured Urghur weapons.

They looked at Brady as their standard, the perfect soldier to emulate. Invincible in their eyes, he was their view of perfection.

Feeling particularly proud of them, he felt total confidence they would perform under pressure in any dicey situations.

Their goal on this day was to find that main nest and the queen. Leading his group of fifty, he wanted enough force to cope if they were surprised by an Urghur patrol, but not enough troops to draw unusual notice from the enemy. It was an arbitrary choice of numbers Brady made, a guess.

They moved single file until they left friendly lands and got into territories far more in question. Fanning out in groups of five, they carefully eased ahead to avoid detection. The kinds of traps the Urghur set had never changed, so Brady trusted his troops to be able to avoid any snares.

The farther along they went, the more of those snares they encountered. It slowed their progress, but that wasn't the problem for Brady. He was far more interested in locating their goal, the main nest, without setting off alarms. It was dangerous. If one of the enemy soldiers discovered them, all of the enemy would know.

With the small group walking with Brady, the most skilled scout suddenly signaled by raising his fist. The group quickly and quietly left the path just before a very large Urghur patrol passed through.

Immediately, Brady wondered if they were approaching their quarry. The size of this enemy force far exceeded any patrol they'd ever encountered. Whether they were patrolling or on their way to some other assignment, he could only guess. A force of that size wouldn't seem to be a routine patrol.

When they'd finally passed through, his men started to move back to the path, but something struck Brady as odd, so he signaled that they continue to wait in concealment. Before long, a second huge force went along the same path, but they turned to go in a different direction. They were soon followed by a third large force. Any one of those groups greatly outnumbered Brady's fifty troops. Having a battle was not an option here, and now that the Urghurs were behind him, a quick escape was ruled out. It had to be a cautious retreat when they left.

Slowly coming back onto the path, they inched forward, but the troops soon hustled back out of sight numerous times, as significant numbers of enemy patrols popped up frequently. Patrols of this size further caused Brady to assume they were in the right place.

Calling on the radio to alert the main base to tag this area for later aerial recon and possible attack, Brady shared his opinion with the colonel.

"I can't say for sure, but this site has all of the signs we'd expect from the area around the main nest," he whispered. "We're seeing significant enemy troop activity."

While they waited, the continuing movement of enemy troops left them in severe jeopardy, even while in concealment. Soon, remote controlled allied drones overflew the area, though they merely filmed the scene. However, the enemy troops slunk out of sight. It was easy to see that the Urghur had learned about the effects of allied air superiority and had adapted, taking appropriate steps so as not to reveal the strength of their presence there.

Those flights increasingly drew in Urghur forces from the surrounding areas in a defensive configuration. Brady suddenly realized he and his men were trapped in an area teeming with Urghurs. It was pure luck none of his men was discovered as some Urghur soldiers came very close to the allied hiding spots.

However, in spite of the terrible risk, it was impossible to draw back away to safer ground. They were frozen in place, hoping for continued good luck in avoiding detection.

As he watched the enemy troops, Brady noted that many of these seemed to be younger, smaller Urghur. If they were newly matured hatchlings, it would explain a lot.

As always, being close to them was a fright. Even their normal sounds were intimidating. Their clicks and various ululations was possibly a language, but it didn't register on his universal translator.

Meal time for them was considerable raw meat brought out from their bases, which they attacked with vigor. Whether the meat came from animals, or other beings like captured Akara, they couldn't tell. Mercifully, there were no living beings or animals slaughtered in front of them. Still, it was a gruesome sight.

Brady and his unit took sips of water and downed some dried meat and cubes of cheese while they waited. There was nothing else they could do at that point except wait and maintain their strength.

The large collection of Urghur troops did not dissipate quickly, which meant Brady and his men were trapped there for the night. Larger-sized Urghur soldiers, who had been patrolling abroad, returned and passed through the area. Brady mentally noted where they all went.

Although the troop movement was like a signal beacon pointing them to their goal, going there was virtually impossible. The danger of detection was far too great already, even with being stationary.

They were in an area of thicker forest and heavy undergrowth. If the Urghur had picked this place as the site of their queen's nest, it was easy to see why. However, verifying it to be certain seemed beyond them. It left Brady with a guess as to exact location of the nest entrance, with no concrete proof.

Actually, escaping safely seemed another near-to-impossible task. Brady pondered what to do. Having the fleet available, he could have called down planet-buster salvos to devastate this area, but that option didn't exist any longer.

His second serious concern was that the Urghur seemed in the process of rapidly replenishing their horde with new births who matured into soldiers. Since the allies' supply of ammo was dwindling, that was a development which could not be allowed, or else a new wave of slaughter and horror could potentially wipe out the allies, including all of the people of the Akara nation. Primitive weapons would not stem the tide against renewed Urghur numbers.

"Come on, Brady, think," he muttered in helpless frustration. A mental image of Beca caught and savaged in the mandibles of an Urghur killer flitted through his mind to punish him. It evoked his deep rage and his determination to prevail in this test.

Turning to his Akara lieutenant, he whispered, "In spite of the risk, in the night, we're going to slip out of here. Not only are we going to escape, we're not going to tip them off we're here."

"Yes, sir." The Akara warriors simply accepted whatever he said. Their total faith in him was a little disconcerting, like miracles were routine.

Brady pondered. *What will they think the first time something goes wrong? Sooner or later, something always goes wrong.*

An Urghur patrol passed dangerously close. Again, it was a miracle they avoided notice. The sky was darkening, so decreased light helped them to survive the frightening moment.

Later, when it was completely dark, Brady started to move. His people were silent as they followed. This was the high-danger moment. Although darkness obscured their movements, it also obscured any Urghur troops around them. Stumbling into sentries was a real possibility as they had to avoid any fights.

It was a nerve-racking time as they edged slowly along. Each step had to be taken cautiously, as every tree, bough, or bush could harbor an enemy. Fortunately, the additional risk of predators hunting at night was reduced, because the animals avoided the Urghur troops. In addition to herbivores, the Urghur ate predator animals too.

The stress affected Brady, but he held up under the strain on behalf of his troops; he did not want to let them down. Obviously, the additional incentive of staying alive factored in also.

Regardless, it was incredibly difficult, among the toughest treks he'd ever taken. Even as they inched along, no matter how far they went, they had no way of knowing when they were out of imminent danger. Each sound around them in the dark was frightening.

After hours on the move, Brady led his unit into a thicket area to rest.

"Is everybody okay?" he whispered. He received murmured whispers in response.

It was a fortuitous stop, as a sizeable Urghur force moved past them going toward the nest. The allies were too close to the path, so none of them dared to move.

It was amazing, with how physically large the Urghur soldiers were, how soundlessly they could move. Brady's group would have stumbled straight into a deadly battle where they would have been outnumbered; it would have become a killing field, and the end of all of them in a matter of mere moments.

The near miss rattled Brady.

This enemy troop was hauling a considerable load of fresh animal kills to help feed the swarm. Brady couldn't help thinking he and his crew could easily have been a part of the food delivery to the nest.

It took a time before the enemy troop completely passed by before Brady cautiously edged back out onto the small path. They continued their progress away from the peril, but still, they didn't feel safe, nor did they dare let their guard down.

Brady's lieutenant edged up close behind him. "That was frightening," he whispered.

"We're still here, that's what's important. The risk was worth it, because now we have an idea of where we need to attack."

"Yes, sir."

Brady glanced back and smiled. "Have I told you how proud we in the corps are to serve with you and the other Akara brethren?"

"Yes."

Brady smiled, as the Akara were still a very literal people and missed many human nuances of speech and mannerism.

"You've done so much more than we could have hoped for against this deadly enemy. I don't want to sound overconfident, because we have no reason to be. We're still in terrible jeopardy, and the war can go either way. However, I can honestly say that I feel some hope for us, all of us."

"Thank you, sir. We trust you implicitly."

"My hope for the future is getting you to the point where you put trust in each other. Yes, E3T got you started, but you're carrying the ball now. Your nation is more than capable of your own defense."

He smiled with pride. "I want to believe that."

"Survival is a strong incentive to do whatever you must. With your women starting to take up the sword, it's a good thing to show your true nature."

"Beca has become a shining beacon for us. It's like she is one of you rather than an Akara."

"She's definitely Akara, but I think of her as the wave of the future. Having competent females is a good thing."

"We're coming to understand that, sir. Do you consider her for being your mate?"

"Eh . . . I'm not considering anybody to be my mate."

"Among us, it's well known she favors you, and perhaps you're the only male worthy of her."

Brady just shook his head, but he grinned. Even about that matter, he was evolving.

Chapter Seven

The harrowing retreat, although very lengthy and seemingly too slow, finally passed as they returned to familiar territory. Even though they were safer, Brady waited until they re-entered the cave and made their way down into the city before he radioed the main E3T base. Everybody in his crew remained on edge, as the strain of this recon mission had taken an emotional toll. Frightening missions weren't so easy to forget mentally, even for experienced troops.

"These are the approximate coordinates of the queen's nest. From what I observed, new hatchlings are already taking places in their military forces. I'm of the opinion we have a narrow window to make a move before their numbers become too great for us to conquer with the restricted amount of ammo we have left."

"I don't disagree," Colonel Severn replied. "I'm going to look at our options and then get back with you shortly. We're still looking for other caches of supplies, just in case there are any to be found."

"That would be a great asset. I gather communications back home are still silent."

"Somebody there has a big problem they want to cover up. We're pawns caught in the wrong place at the wrong time."

"It makes me sick. Expendable in battle is something we understand when we sign up, but being sacrificial lambs for their screw-ups, that doesn't fly with me. Are they so insulated they're immune to any consequences? Can we be that corrupt?"

"I suspect the corruption goes very high up, maybe all the way to the top. This has been true for a very long time. In my opinion, it goes to the root of every species, having fallible natures. In my experiences, it seems to be universal. Making honest mistakes is much different than cold calculations where they factor in their version of acceptable loss. Now we're a part of the acceptable loss of this mission."

"It's funny. I mentioned to my friends that I wondered who was telling the generals and admirals what to do. Maybe they are the culprits."

"Possibly, but I suspect there are background, shadowy figures pulling the strings. Generals and admirals probably aren't creative enough people to concoct these devious plans. They aren't motivated by the same things. Greed is more the province and expertise of civilian folk."

"You might be right, although ascribing greater moral fiber to military folk is probably wrong."

"I know. I'm not saying generals and admirals can't be bribed and bought off, but their price would be pretty low compared to what the vile people pay in bribes to civilians. It's probably just a drop in their bucket and well within acceptable parameters for their seamy operations."

"Maybe we can convince the Urghur horde to invade headquarters."

Colonel Severn chuckled. "Right, Brady."

"What surprises me is that lower-level people, people who know us and are our friends, don't do something about this."

"If those friends don't know we're alive because our messages are jammed or interdicted by the bad guys, then that's your answer."

"If, through some miracle, we survive this, I'm making it my mission to go after those bastards."

"I understand the sentiment, Brady, but we need to focus on the more immediate task at hand. In addition to the growing problem of dealing with the horde, their home world forces could reappear at any time."

"You're right, sir. I worry about that too. It's strange they suddenly cut off their transport lines. We have no way of knowing what happened on their end, so we have no way to anticipate what's ahead for us."

"Dealing with our present situation is all we can do. If the worst happens, we take as many of them down with us as we can. Giving the Akara nation the best chance possible to survive is the best we can do."

"I think the Akara people aren't interested in going back to their old life under the boot of the Urghur horde. They will fight to the last soul, with the understanding that it may not matter how many Urghur soldiers are killed, with queens just pumping out more births. Basically, there is a near-endless supply of reinforcements on their side."

"That's a sobering reality."

"It is, sir. Are you married?"

"Yes, I left a wife and two sons behind. We couldn't join the evacuation due to the particular circumstances in our region. Unlike you, I didn't choose to be the rear guard."

"I'm sorry to hear that."

"Sadly, I wasn't surprised when the fleet made a prompt exit."

"I don't know what to say. Obviously, we're all angry, but it's being helpless to do anything about it that's so frustrating. If we're marooned here, but we have sufficient supplies to have a life, I look at it differently. Do you see what I'm saying? With the limits on ammo, I worry we'll be sitting ducks before too long a time."

"I understand completely."

"Well, enough of my complaining. I'll let you go, Colonel. Thanks for listening."

"Brady, we're all in the same boat. Anytime you need to talk, I'm happy to listen. I might be calling you to vent someday."

Brady was surprised when he turned around to see Beca standing nearby, listening to the somber conversation.

"Are you distressed because you can't go home?"

"Yes, to an extent."

"Are you sorry you're stranded here with my people?"

"It has nothing to do with your people, Beca. If you don't understand we truly care about you, there's no way I could explain it. As I said, having sufficient materials to survive and flourish, that's what I mean. Using captured Urghur weapons is better than nothing, but not the optimal situation."

"Did I mention that my next younger sisters, Sira and Wyla, are joining the next class of females going into training in the war arts?"

"What do your parents say about it?"

"They accept it. I think what I've accomplished has changed their minds. Also, I think all of my people understand finally that it's a new world now and we must adapt. Resisting change serves no good purpose. You're not alone in realizing that more Urghurs could reappear from off-world at any time. We'll give them our utmost effort in the war. If our race must die out, we won't go quietly."

Suddenly swept with emotion at the appalling possibility she'd stated, Beca stepped close to hug Brady. It surprised him, and after a moment he returned her hug.

"Beca, we'll do our best to be sure that doesn't happen. The corps never gives up."

It took her a moment before she composed herself and stepped back. "I understand so much better now. I can see how the Akara seem like such children to you. We were so ignorant in our simple life. There was an entire universe all around us that we knew nothing about. In the ancient days, the fact there was terrible danger close at hand never occurred to us in our complacency. Therefore, we weren't prepared when they came. Living in ignorance in our stodgy ways was no protection. Being faithful to Akara precepts and tenets was only important in the foolishness of our minds.

"We subscribed to the teachings and followed the leadership of councils of old men who we called holy. I see the end result of that folly. I'm ashamed of our history. I'm ashamed we acceded to Urghur domination and abuse with barely a whisper, as if by turning our heads away, the horror wasn't happening and would simply go away. With whatever fallacies you think your people have, it pales in comparison to the colossal blunders of the Akara."

"Beca, don't."

"Why? Why not? Is anything I'm saying untrue? Would it not have been better to die in the beginning, fighting them to the death? Was it better to be nothing more than their food for all of these ages?"

"I know it's a tough pill to swallow."

"I tell you this. I'm proud of my two sisters. I'm glad they're joining the training. If we can never conquer and destroy these vile creatures, at least now we'll take a terrible toll on them."

"I—"

"Don't bother. I would rather you act toward me now like you do with Misty and Sara."

"Okay, I can do that."

"I will also say, since you seem to barely realize it, Misty and Sara hold you fondly in their hearts. I think you don't fully understand that. You say none of you wish to take a mate while you are soldiers. I don't think everybody agrees with you. I won't tell you what they say in private. I don't hide the fact of what I want. That won't change. If you ever wish to talk to me further about this, I'm always ready."

Brady was at a loss for words. For him, that topic was a slippery slope. Taking a first step could lead to . . . challenges.

"I don't require a reply." Beca smiled ruefully, turned her back to walk away, and took a step.

"Beca, wait. I want to tell you I value you and your entire people. I can't really say that's ever been true for me before. I'm sure it isn't what you want to hear, but for me, it's a big realization."

Turning her head back, she eyed him thoughtfully. "Thank you, Brady."

Watching her walk away, Brady realized also that she was now a significant woman in his life. It was another first. What to do was another question altogether. He no longer had that inner feeling of her as an alien and was surprised at how quickly it had dissipated. Although it was seemingly a gradual transition in his mind, regardless, it was another first for Brady that it had happened at all.

Standing in a momentary stupor of contemplation before he was interrupted by Rosca, he frowned, out of his element, facing unfamiliar emotions.

"Brady, is something wrong?"

"No, I . . . eh . . ."

"We've discussed our situation among ourselves, the council and the leaders. It's the most difficult choice in our history, because if we commit to all-out war against the Urghur, with the risk of our total annihilation, our long history as a race could come to an end by choices we make. Extinction . . . it's a very sobering possibility. I believe you understand. We're talking for more than just our fighters. We're talking for all the Akara women and children and the unborn Akara of the future."

"I do understand. I wish there was a viable alternative option, but we both know at this point that the new Urghur hatchlings will mature, and then they will be relentless in ferreting out all Akara hiding places. You're right, there are no good options. Total annihilation will apply to us also. We're invested in your survival and the ultimate defeat of the Urghur army too. We've just got to find a way. I know I say the same things, but Echo Three Tango isn't a force that goes out quietly, no matter the challenges."

Rosca smiled. "Your determination encourages us. It's a great trait for us to emulate. We've never felt confidence about dealing with the enemy."

They both paused a moment, pondering the difficult task.

"I saw you talking to Beca?"

"She's remarkable on so many levels. She put it out there to me about an 'us,' but I'm at a loss. She already knows where I'm coming from, but honestly, it's an appealing idea. If this is the end of the line for me, maybe I should think about taking a wife, even if the marriage is very short."

"The Akara people would be honored to have you join the family of the people."

"That honor would be all mine, if it happened."

"Are you aware your females are being deluged with proposals from Akara males?"

"I had heard that. I don't think our warrior ladies are onboard with getting married, though. Maybe they'll change their minds. I can't speak for them."

"Nonetheless, I suspect our young men see the same dim ending that we do. They also want to experience that aspect of life, even if it is brief."

"As I said, I'm not going to speak for the ladies. They make their own choices about everything."

"Coming back to the issue at hand, have you decided on specific plans and battle strategies? As you said, waiting only makes them stronger."

"I have not, but I wouldn't be the one making an overall battle plan. I'll let the colonel take that responsibility. He's supposed to get back in touch with me. I think he has a similar dilemma. With our finite ammo supplies, we also have the all-or-nothing issues. If we attack without hitting that nest and getting the queen, obviously at that point we become vulnerable. If we're left only with captured Urghur weapons and your primitive weapons, that is a recipe for disaster. The biggest loss would be the superiority our air forces give us. They're more than an equalizer. They're the game changer and the key to surviving the war."

Rosca frowned. "So much bad news, it's difficult to digest. I try to be optimistic for our people, but in my heart, I'm very worried."

"This isn't a time to sugarcoat the problem. Each of us in this alliance must accept the reality of our own possible demise, but more importantly, we must use the fact that we're the last line of defense to motivate us to achieve more than we think is possible."

"Yes, that's it exactly. Our ladies in training want to be a part of the fight."

"I leave that choice to you and your military staff. At this point, Beca's trainee class is more than capable. The newer ones have a way to go before they're ready to go to war."

"Let me know when you hear from the colonel. In the meantime, I'm going to pass the word throughout our forces, here and everywhere else, to be prepared to move at a moment's notice."

"I will."

Brady went to find his old unit friends. Misty and Sara were having a quick snack, while Bontag and Jocol were just returning with a patrol.

Brady nodded to the men and motioned them over. They all joined the two women seated at a table and shared in having a lunchtime meal.

"I do like this local berry wine," said Bontag.

"It's very good," Misty remarked. "The alcohol content must be lower. It's warming without knocking you out."

"It's one of the few good things coming from this planet," Sara added.

They all looked at Brady. Sara continued, "I gather you've got something to say?"

"I just wanted to take a moment for us. For some reason, I have this feeling we have something really big at hand. With our difficult situation, I can't be sure of the outcome. So, just in case, I want to say it's been an honor to know and serve with every one of you and to be companions. If this is my end, I can't think of a better group of people I want to have around me. Ladies, what you've done in bringing those Akara women along to battle readiness is nothing short of amazing."

"They always had it in them," Misty answered reflectively. "We were facilitators, but given the chance, they could have done it on their own."

"That's okay, Misty. You don't need to be humble. It's just us here, and we all know the truth. The colonel is working out a strategy and a plan, but our idea to take out the main nest and the queen, it's iffy at best. If we open up there with our aircraft ordnance and don't hit the right spot, or don't do damage deep enough to get her, you know what happens next."

He looked at four grim stares. None of them were full of optimism. Reality was not a thing one could simply dismiss.

"We need a miracle," Bontag muttered.

"In the past, the corps has always made our own miracles. I wish we had adequate ammo reserves."

"Well, we don't, Brady."

"So, do you have any ideas? What you're saying is the obvious."

"I don't have some genius plan. I just wanted this quiet time to be with you guys. Once it all breaks loose, and that could happen very soon, we may not get any more time. I look at you as family."

"So, is this a 'get your affairs in order' gathering?"

"It's more like a 'come to Jesus' moment, Misty," said Jocol. "We may never gather together again as a group in this life. Our next meeting might be in the next life."

Sara added, "It's funny, for as many times as we've gone into battle and faced some near misses, I never thought about checking out. It was always there as a possibility, but I never dwelled on it. Right now, I feel like Brady. Something is different, and not in a good way. Those Urghur aren't stupid. They'll know what our only goal will need to be, so you're right. If they mislead us to hit the wrong place and use up the ordnance, the chess game becomes purely defensive for us. Either we run and hide for as long as we can, or we make it a suicide attack, no turning back. Fight to the last living soul. I think about all of the innocent Akara women and children all over this planet. It will be a nightmare of epic proportions, being defenseless against the slaughter. The Urghur don't have pity or mercy. I don't even know if they have feelings in our sense of the word."

Brady uttered, "It's funny to me how it messes with my mind. Beca pretty much said she wants to marry me . . . now. I got what she was saying. If the battle goes bad, she doesn't want to die without having experienced marriage and love. I have to admit, it made me think."

"We've all had some thoughts along that line," said Misty. "Sara and I have really become targets lately for the Akara warriors' romantic attention. I wouldn't call it courting, because of the positions we've taken, but they're driven in getting us to notice their wishes."

She looked at Sara, who added, "It is very flattering. None of us have really looked seriously in that direction. Going out without experiencing that part of life, I do understand what Beca is saying. What are you going to do, Brady? You know Misty and I have wondered about if you'd consider either of us in that role."

Brady got a distant look.

Bontag suddenly spoke. "Since we're baring our souls, I think I can speak for Jocol when I say, we've thought about you ladies also. Granted, we're both of different races, so maybe that would be too much of an impediment in your minds."

"Of course not, Bontag," Sara replied. "You're both appealing, potential mates, although in different ways."

"What are we saying?" asked Jocol. "Are we pondering having a big night before the battle starts?"

The five all laughed.

"I don't know if you meant that as a joke," said Brady. "For my part, I wasn't trying to organize an orgy or something like that. For me, it would be actually getting married to somebody."

"Likewise," said the women.

Jocol continued, "If I wanted to marry, I've got a very limited pool of candidates on this planet. None of these little Akara women would survive a wedding night with me. Our two human ladies here might be strong enough, though. Mating in my species is a near feral process. Once we go into that reproductive mode, we become . . . motivated out of our minds and lose control to an extent. Our females are strong enough to survive it, and they have their own version of the frenzy. We evoke each other. Do you understand?"

"Wow, that was romantic," said Misty.

Again, the group chuckled.

"I'm just being honest."

"Duly noted."

"I can grasp what all of you are saying and what you feel. I know I'm seen as this hulking savage, not husband material."

Misty looked at Sara. "Jocol, I'm not saying you're wrong in how you're perceived, but I think you see it in far more negative terms than reality. Every one of us rejoices in being your companion. On the battlefield, there isn't another living being we'd rather have at our side. As far as being a husband, I think Sara would agree, it would be an interesting challenge to find compromises that would work for both sides. Don't think you couldn't be considered in that role."

"I . . ."

"Jocol, at a loss for words? I never thought I'd see the day," said Brady.

The group laughed, and Jocol smiled broadly. In his case, his smile came across as threatening to those unfamiliar with his species. The E3T members knew better and understood his mannerisms.

"Thank you, Misty. It means a great deal to me to have your respect and compassion."

Brady resumed, "Coming back to the issue at hand, what I'm saying is whatever each of us individually decides to do, it's okay. There is no judgment, or other factors, to impede taking your personal steps. As far as if anybody is looking to connect with an Akara person, before getting close, I leave it to you to honor their rules and to discuss it with their families. I wouldn't anticipate problems from them, because they worship us."

The group was quiet, pondering possibilities.

Brady added, "You understand why I'm saying this now. The high probability is we have very little time before it all breaks loose. If you're going to pull the trigger, now is the time."

"We'll think about this, Brady," Sara replied. "It's not an easy decision."

"Agreed, and that's true for the guys as much as the girls."

He looked at all of their faces. "Bontag, you haven't said much."

"I'm also considering this proposition. I feel somewhat like Jocol, like I'm not particularly well suited for these females either. My race has our own distinct ways about mating. Whether Akara females, human women, or the other E3T females in our midst would find compatibility with me is a real question. I'm not unmoved by the desire to have a mate, but the practicality for me is probably more difficult than for Jocol."

"Obviously, we don't understand what you mean, but perhaps it's something you can work out in private with the female of your choice?"

"Perhaps, Brady. However, for me, taking the risk of wooing a female only to be rejected is more daunting than the risk of going into battle. About mating, being rejected, for my race, is devastating to us beyond anything I could describe to you. I know you don't understand because you're a different species. You must simply accept my word; our males are incredibly cautious about taking that step, even with our own women. It virtually must be a sure thing. The damage of a rejection irreparably shatters our feelings of self-worth."

He glanced at Misty and Sara. They were eyeing him thoughtfully.

Sara spoke, "Bontag, we feel affection for you as much as we do for Jocol. However, with human women, we can't prejudge to guarantee to you an acceptance of a serious relationship. We experience it and then make our decisions."

"I understand. This is why I often seem aloof to you. I'm not unmoved by your female allure. I'm just not sure I'm the person to step in to fulfill it. In the area of your word 'love,' failure is not an option for me."

Misty and Sara looked at each other.

Everybody looked at Brady.

"Well, folks, I've said my piece, so at this point the ball is in your court to do whatever, or do nothing, as you see fit. Whether having potentially a very short marriage is a good idea, you've got to decide that for yourselves."

Brady got up and walked away. His own mind was whirring at the difficult thoughts. *Is that a route for me? Misty and Sara are certainly worthy and appealing options. Should I allow myself to consider Beca in such a role?*

Walking out of the cave, he saw a flight from the air base had just landed. Coming up the mountainside was his favorite pilot, Sonya. She was involved in an in-depth discussion with Visule, who had arrived with her. They didn't notice Brady until they nearly bumped into him. He pondered her too. She was another intriguing candidate to be a wife.

"Brady, hello. Sorry we didn't notice you there." Sonya smiled at him. She noticed his thoughtful expression and his intent stare.

"Hi, folks, you seem pretty intense in whatever you're talking about."

Visule answered, "I've come here to be close to the coming action. This is possibly the critical focal point for determining action in the war against the Urghur armies. I'm no tactician, but as I observe how the enemy responds, perhaps I can add valuable insight to help us cope on the fly. This isn't a time for our defeat. There will be no second chances."

"I couldn't agree more. Welcome. I won't hold you up, so go ahead into the cave and down to the city."

Sonya was eyeing Brady closely. "You go ahead, Visule. I'm going to talk to Brady a moment."

Visule nodded and moved on.

"Brady, what's up? You're looking at me strangely."

"Sorry, I just talked with my friends. It kind of blew my mind."

"Talked about what?"

"Well, we've been deluged with offers to . . . well . . . to get married, while we still can. This upcoming desperation battle could be the end for us and it makes me think about things."

"You're talking about Akara offers. I've gotten plenty of those too. I agree; it does make you think. So, are you on the verge of pulling the trigger?"

"My answer would always have been no, but . . . it does make you rethink old ideas. Beca has put it out there, and of course, Misty and Sara have always had a warm spot in my heart."

He glanced at her. "You're certainly a woman to consider about that also."

Sonya chuckled. "Me? Wow, I'm honored, Brady. Do you understand the reverse is true also? We women look at you as a highly desirable candidate."

"I'll take your word for that."

"So, is this a proposal? Do we work in a wedding night on our schedule of things to do?"

They both chuckled.

"I'm sorry to spring this on you out of the blue, Sonya. It's just something we're all pondering. None of us have been in this kind of situation before."

"I'm included. It's something I should have considered too. I guess I've been so busy, with my mind focused on the war."

"Our minds need to be focused on the battle too."

"If I propose to you right now, I'll guarantee Misty and Sara will probably take me down, and probably Beca would help them. I think they won't easily give you up."

"I think the other women have other options, just like you do."

"We have our favorites. You have to decide who you would want."

"I ... eh ..."

"Very profound, Brady."

They chuckled again. "That's not an easy choice, Sonya."

"The one sure thing to keep in mind is that you can't choose us all. The losers will cope but satisfying everybody can't be done."

Chapter Eight

Brady walked with Sonya into the cave, and they headed down the tunnel until they entered the city. The city was bustling with activity, just like in other spots across the globe where the combined allied military forces had gathered and were preparing with a feeling of urgency for the impending battle. Delay was universally acknowledged to be no acceptable option. With each passing day, the Urghur horde grew.

Brady was surprised to see his friends were still together talking. Coincidentally, Beca had noticed him and walked over toward them.

As she arrived at the group, Sonya said, "So, Brady tells me you've been talking about some options, fun options. Judging by how he's acting, I think he's thinking pretty seriously about this. I don't even have a wedding dress handy."

Everybody laughed, including Beca. She spoke, "Is this meeting restricted? Are Akara allowed to join you?"

"Of course you're welcome, Beca," Sonya answered for the group. "You're a player in this game. You've got an equal shot at Brady."

"Hey, what a minute, ladies. I'm not going on the auction block. We're all thinking about the future, so don't make it all about me."

"Well, Brady, it's clear to me, Misty, Sara, and Beca, you're not going to choose, so if we want wedded bliss before the end, we've got to make the move."

"What does that mean?"

The women eyed each other and smirked. He eyed them sheepishly.

"Eh . . . I admit, I did not see that coming. Although you're right, it would be near to impossible for me to choose one of you. Your alternative is . . . well, what is your alternative?"

The ladies laughed.

Misty said, "How do you like feeling like an object? We live with it daily all of our lives because we're women."

"I haven't decided I should do this. If I'm distracted in this battle, it could be a really bad thing. It's nothing against any of you."

"That's true for all of us, Brady. It's true for Jocol and Bontag just as much as you."

"So, is your hypothetical solution going to include them too?"

"Maybe. We haven't really pondered that . . . yet."

"With three guys and four girls in this pool of candidates, that would seem to be a problem in itself."

"I can step away," said Beca.

"No need, Beca," Sara answered. "You're on an equal footing with us, and maybe it's you who Brady favors."

Beca blushed, but then smiled warmly. It made Brady smile. Her exuberance was always intoxicating, and she was still an incredibly appealing female. With her strength work in the training program, she was now sculpted of form and physically fit to near perfection. Arguably now the supreme Akara female in the world in every meaningful way, she had endless romantic possibilities and interest, including E3T personnel.

Jocol was staring at the women, wide-eyed. For him, it was a frightening possibility. In his mind, certainly Beca did not seem to be a viable candidate to survive his wedding night. Sonya seemed possibly slightly less capable than Misty or Sara of the task. All of the women were appealing, but injuring them was not something he was sure he could avoid when lost in the mating frenzy of his people. Exercising necessary restraint and control was near to impossible for his species.

Bontag was glazed-eyed, like this was a surreal moment. That he was part of the mix here was astounding to him. Potentially having one of these superb women as his mate, it was mind boggling and incredibly evocative.

Brady asked, "If we do this, do we make it official, and if so, how?"

Beca replied, "Our priests could perform a ritual. Our joining ceremony is lengthy, but I'm sure they would agree to abbreviate the rites as you direct them."

"Wow, you're making this too easy. Remember that old saying, 'be careful what you wish for.'"

"I can't speak for the other women, but from my perspective, and I realize I'm young, I don't want to die without experiencing that part of life."

"Here, here, Beca," said the other women. Their avid looks at Brady were daunting. He shifted on his feet, feeling awkward.

"I don't know what standing a marriage by our priests would have in your world."

"We have interspecies bonding routinely, so your ceremony would be accepted like any other back home," Misty explained.

"Then I'm ready." Beca's eyes sparkled as she stared at Brady. At that point, it was beyond a daunting moment for him. In essence, in public, in front of the others, she'd put the ball in his court.

Brady glanced at those others to see widespread amused looks. He paused to consider this huge step, when he was interrupted by an Akara warrior suddenly rushing in from the tunnel toward them.

"Come quickly! It's the Urghur."

The group joined the exodus of the curious rushing out of the cave entrance. Once they broke into the open outside, they saw the terrifying view of a huge Urghur army marching their way. Rosca was racing about, issuing commands to the Akara army. Troops were scrambling to deploy to preset positions.

"I've got to get down to my fighter," said Sonya. She raced down the mountain at a dead run without waiting.

Brady turned to his people. "Gear up. It's time to earn our money."

Beca followed them back down the tunnel to arm for battle. Those Akara females who were graduates of the training program gathered around Misty and Sara like they were the command structure rather than the Akara military staff.

Misty said, "Okay ladies, it's our time. Don't try to be a hero or think we can show up the men. There will be death and dying out there. Make sure it's the enemy doing the dying. We don't get into single hand-to-hand with them. They're bigger, stronger, and pitiless. Our weapons are our tools, so stay together, work together, and fight as a unit. Questions?"

Uniformly, their faces were frightened.

"I know how you feel," said Sara. "As I said, working as a unit, and with helping each other, everything will be fine. We can do this. We're protecting your families, way of life, and your right to exist."

The women gave a martial shout. The look in their eyes showed they were focused on the task at hand.

Racing back out of the cave, the women joined the flood of Akara troops streaming down the hillside. By now, the Urghurs had begun their bloodcurdling war cries. It was no less frightening than ever for Brady, or anybody else.

They moved into their preset defensive arrays, designed with overlapping fields of firing patterns. It was a similar strategy to what the original E3T attack plan had been, one which had failed. However, in this case, Brady recognized quickly as the enemy troops got closer that these weren't all mature enemy fighters. Many appeared to be immature, smaller, inexperienced, and barely of an age to be effective fighters.

As Brady positioned the troops around him, keeping the female Akara troops nearby, suddenly they were surprised by Visule, who came rushing up to him.

"Brady, wait; I must tell you something. I think the Urghurs may be in the same dilemma as you. I think they also have limited weaponry and ammo. I don't believe they have factories on this world to create additional supplies. Whether this changes your tactics, I have no idea, but I thought you needed to know before the battle starts."

"Thank you, Visule, that's good to know. Get back up into the cave. You're not expendable, so you need to stay safe."

"I feel guilty for not doing my part in battle while my countrymen die to protect us."

"Your part is not being a grunt. Your part is using your special brain."

Visule hesitated before he finally ascended the mountainside.

"So, do we change tactics?" asked Misty.

"Pass the word to be sure we gather every single Urghur weapon we can and their ammo packs. If we survive long enough, and if it comes down to hand-to-hand combat, that's not necessarily an advantage for us. They're still physically superior, although the immature ones are a better matchup. Jocol is the physical match of any Urghur, but we only have him from his race in our little army."

The allies waited in their defensive positions as the enemy army approached. Their terrifying chant was no less daunting as they drew close.

Brady glanced at the Akara females. There were approximately fifty in their unit. Every one of them looked scared, but they had determined looks in their eyes.

He edged over to Beca, their highest-ranking female. "Are you okay?"

"I'm frightened, but I'll do my duty."

"I want you to stay close to me. Getting through your first battle alive is more important than thinking you need to race out to personally fight in close-quarter combat to prove something. They have the edge in that situation. Don't let your friends lose their heads and act crazy, okay?"

"Certainly. We won't embarrass you."

"I'm not talking about cowardice; I'm talking about not getting killed. These enemy troops are vile. They literally eat those they kill or capture. Keep your ladies back in a support status this first time out."

"Yes, Brady, we understand."

"If we have success, we'll try to move fast, just in case they have a second wave in the area, and strip away the weapons and ammo off their dead."

"We'll be there."

"Good."

They stared at each other for a moment before she suddenly gave him a quick hug. "Brady, you stay alive too."

"I'll try. I always do."

The enemy approached them, racing at full speed in a charge, and hit the first line of allied defenders with a sudden, point-blank, devastating salvo of weapons on both sides, but it only happened once. Seeing this, Brady believed Visule's observation, as the Urghur soldiers appeared to be conserving ammo as much as the allies.

The Akara bravely stood their ground. Their defensive array was situated in tier after tier of troops. For perhaps the first time,

Brady noted the Urghur didn't have a numeral advantage in fighters.

Just as the Urghur were about to attempt one of their normal battle strategies, rotating units in a wheel movement to flank the defenders, Sonya appeared from above and dived downward in her fighter jet, strafing the enemy troops with devastating fire. Those in open ground were mowed down in moments. Sonya then fired on the tree line where the Urghurs tried to retreat out of harm's way. It didn't work out well for the enemy soldiers.

Brady signaled his army into action, and with a mighty roar, they attacked *en masse*.

The female corps did as they were instructed and concentrated on disarming the Urghur dead. The male troops joined their efforts as the vital war materials were gathered up and quickly sent up the mountainside and into the cave.

Meanwhile, the allied attack reached the tree line where the Urghur survivors waited to make their stand. Here, the air superiority couldn't help the allies. It was the deadliest type of fighting against these enemies. Even with greatly reduced numbers, their ferocity remained high. Whether that was courage or the fact they weren't beings with any similarities to humanoids, Brady didn't know. It didn't matter. This was kill or be killed for both sides.

Jocol took the lead, like a spear point of the assault. He was like a scythe harvesting wheat. The preponderance of younger Urghur troops here played into his hands. They neither had the great size nor the battle experience to cope with Jocol. Dying in battle didn't seem to be a factor to them, which was a strange element for the allied side to comprehend.

The young Urghurs tried to plow into Jocol to overwhelm and pull him down, but he was supported by numerous Akara warriors close at hand, so even the Akara were having success. The Urghur's ill-thought strategy failed miserably.

Regardless, it was still a difficult battle, which went on for hours. As always, the Urghur fighters never retreated and never surrendered. Fighting to the death was their only option in every battle.

Although the allies persevered and fought doggedly, they didn't go unscathed. Too many times, allied fighters went down and were quickly taken into the mandibles of the enemy soldiers before those creatures could be killed. It was a horrifying scene to witness.

The female Akara troops were close by in their support and reinforcement duties, so they saw everything. It was a meat grinder of a battle that left mental scars in addition to physical wounds.

At long last, Brady led the best of his troops against the tight knot of the Urghur leaders. They were surrounded in a tight circle by mature fierce troops. Jocol attacked fearlessly, but he was in danger immediately.

"Come on guys, let's end this right here," Brady shouted.

Bontag, Misty, and Sara went shoulder to shoulder with Brady as he surged into the melee around Jocol. Akara warriors roared in a deafening shout and attacked too.

In the middle of this terrible, final assault, Brady was shocked when Beca suddenly appeared beside him in the fighting. The other females joined their men, and it was a significant factor. The women realized they couldn't physically compete with these fully mature Urghur, so their strategy was close quarter, point-blank firing of captured Urghur weapons to take them out. It was a deciding factor in this final stand.

Brady and Jocol got to the leader of the Urghur at the same moment. He was a huge, fierce brute of solid muscle, bulging eyes, and seemingly no neck. His impending death had no meaning to him. He grabbed an Akara soldier, who had gotten too close, and killed him in his mandibles in a sickening crunch of body and bones.

This incensed the E3T, and Jocol in particular. He grabbed the monster in a chokehold while Brady fired a weapon directly into the body.

The monster went down in a heap.

Looking up, Brady saw Beca was beside him with tears in her eyes as she looked at the remains of the slaughtered Akara soldiers.

Brady looked around and saw the few remaining Urghur soldiers were going down from withering, point-blank fire from enraged Akara troops.

When the last one was killed, Brady put an arm around Beca. "Are you okay?"

"No, it was horrible. Seeing what they do, it is something I can never forget."

"I understand. Let's clean up the rest of the weapons and ammo. The animal predators will take care of the dead Urghur bodies tonight."

"Yes," she replied softly. Turning and going to her sisters-in-arms, the ladies got busy in doing their jobs, helping collect the remaining weapons and ammo.

Later, back in the cave, Brady, Misty, and Sara gathered the Akara female corps, both those fifty who'd gone into combat for the first time, and the large number of those still in training. They sat down together on the ground, eyeing Brady intently.

"Ladies, I think now you understand better about battle. I can explain it until I turn blue, but it's not something that can be explained. When you experience it, nothing can prepare you for such horror. War is the worst activity that living beings can do. Unfortunately, often we aren't given a choice about it. Our enemy is relentless and will never stop coming for us. Therefore, we have no choice but to wipe them out. Surviving is more than goal number one. It's the only goal we can have.

"Assuming we do that, the next obstacle is coping with what happens to an individual who is forced to kill. Believe me; the rationalizations we make to excuse taking lives aren't always effective. Saying we had no choice still doesn't assuage feelings of guilt. Sometimes in a fight, you make decisions and do things you're not proud of. Rage can cause any of us to do things for revenge. Maybe you've just seen a comrade die. After the dust has settled, then you think back and need to find a way to live with what you did. Do you understand what I'm saying?"

"I do," said Beca. She stood and turned to face her sisters. "When I saw one of our men die in the jaws of . . ." She had to pause, struggling with her emotions. "I know what Brady is saying. I felt it at that moment, such hatred as I've never experienced before. I wanted to kill that Urghur, but more, I wanted to tear it apart so it died horribly too. At that moment, I didn't think like a little female. I was a soldier of the Akara people."

The entire female group gave a martial shout. Their courageous response gave Brady chills down his spine.

"I'm sorry, Brady," Beca continued. "I didn't mean to interrupt your remarks."

"Beca, it's fine. You said it eloquently, exactly what I was trying to say."

"We weren't naïve about war, but you're right. No imagining could have prepared us for that. It gives me great respect for what our men have done for centuries. What they have faced out there, it's a heavy burden."

"It is that."

"What do you think about our chances?"

"Well, as you all saw, it was fortuitous we own the skies. With her intervention, Sonya put us in the position to win. Even with her culling their ranks, it was still a difficult battle. I don't know if we would have won. If we project ahead, imagine closing in on the main nest to get the queen. If we've used up our air ordnance, I don't know what happens at that point. This was a battle with mostly immature Urghur troops, and they pressed us to the limit. How many mature, full-strength Urghur soldiers are guarding the queen? We have no idea."

"Do we have another choice? I thought we established that's our only viable option, if we wish to survive."

"I can't disagree, Beca. I'm just talking about getting false illusions or unwarranted optimism."

"That's not a problem. We fully understand the reality of our situation. We've lived with these things all of our lives."

"Again, if our strategy is to commit the entire Akara nation into a final, pitched battle to destroy the nest and the queen, getting everybody moved there from all across the planet is a difficult problem to solve. That would be an all-or-nothing risk, with no guarantee of a victory in the end. Instead, it could be a self-inflicted, extinction-level event."

Misty added, "The Urghur know that end-game scenario too. We can be sure they're preparing for our most probable tactic. Running out of ammo is far less a problem for them than for us. They haven't needed to set traps up until now, because they haven't been on the defensive. Because we think of them as misbegotten mistakes of nature doesn't mean they aren't intelligent and capable of being dangerous in their strategies too. That attack we just experienced may be their way of letting us know that they know where we're hiding. Sacrificing immature, less-able fighters to draw our fire weakens us, not them. Every round we fire from the weapons, on the ground or in the air, helps the Urghur. Casualties are not a concern for them if we're rendered vulnerable and can rely only on primitive weapons."

Brady picked up. "We have huge numbers of people in the Akara nation. If their casualties have culled them to the point of tipping the scales in our favor, we have no way to know. How fast their queen can breed functional replacements is the x-factor. How long it takes new hatchlings to grow and mature, we also don't know. Those younger ones we just killed, they may have hatched months ago, weeks ago, or maybe days ago."

"With all of this bad news, is there any good news?" asked Beca.

"I wish I had an answer. It's not like we can infiltrate a spy into the nest to find out for sure."

"You don't believe bombing the nest will be the answer, do you?"

"Well, if the fleet was still overhead, our planet busters would definitely take out the nest, no matter how deep it is in the ground. However, the explosives on our fighter craft aren't designed for deep penetrations into the ground. Their function in our battles is in supporting the ground assaults and culling enemy troops and degrading their defensive positions."

"So, is it a mistake for us to attack the Urghur armies?"

"That is one of those questions with a complicated answer. The answer may be yes on both sides of the equation. Yes, it's a mistake to expose our people to terrible risk by attacking their strongest position, and yes, we must do it anyway."

Beca frowned. "Since we have no other viable choice, we prepare for the inevitable. I hope afterwards there is still an Akara nation."

"Amen," said Brady sadly.

The meeting broke up, with the Akara women wandering off to seek out their families. Beca came over to Brady. "Would you come with me to visit my family?"

"Okay. Was there something you needed for me to do?"

"No. I've already spoken my wishes. It isn't necessary to repeat them. This is just sharing your time with us, a family that cares about you a great deal."

"Thank you. I'll come with you."

Misty and Sara watched them walk away together. Brady almost stopped to tell them this wasn't some decision on his part, that spending time with Beca was a pleasantry, not a marriage proposal. But it dawned on him immediately how verbalizing that would needlessly embarrass Beca, so he let it slide and continued walking away at her side.

Even with his going with her, Brady did notice the sad look on her face.

When they arrived at her parent's hut, the parents were sitting outside, talking with the other four daughters.

"Beca," said her mother, "it's so good to see you."

"Hello, Mother." The women embraced. Beca's two youngest sisters came over to hug her also.

"Hi, little monkeys."

"Beca, you're famous. The people talk about you like you're one of them," said little Senni.

"I'm no different than any other Akara person. I try to do my duty to defend the people, nothing more."

"The people are proud about you and him."

Beca smiled. "You can stop with that kind of talk. Brady and I aren't . . . together."

"Not yet," said Miran, the next-oldest sister. The youngsters smiled impishly and snickered.

Beca smiled. "Okay, we didn't come here to get silly about things, young ladies."

Her parents had been eyeing Brady closely for his reactions. He tried to show no reactions at all. However, he felt self-internalized pressure to make a decision on the spot.

Nearby, Sira and Wyla had been watching too, but with distracted looks. They focused their total attention only when the little girls broached the issue of Beca snagging Brady, at which point they showed curious looks. Everybody eyed him closely at the matrimonial prospect being spoken out loud, and in front of the whole family. They waited for him to respond.

Brady shifted on his feet, feeling awkward. He pondered, *This isn't a forum to air my inner feelings, is it?* He wasn't even sure about those inner feelings.

Finally, Beca broke the awkward silence. "Well, perhaps we should have a quick meal, Mother."

"Of course, I'm sorry. Please come into the hut, Brady. It's nice to have you back for a visit."

When Brady sat down, Miran sat on one side and Senni on his other side. Beca sat beside her father. She looked at anybody but Brady.

The conversation was light; mostly the youngest daughters related their daily activities and schooling highlights. It was a pleasant and relaxing time. This was the joy of family, the close bond between siblings. It was no different than Brady's own family had been with his two little sisters.

Unfortunately for the two other sisters, the older ones in training, they felt this moment was the calm before the storm. The call from the colonel back at the main base could come at any time and the horror of the great battle could commence. Their worry reflected in their expressions and short sentences.

Brady talked with the little girls, but his battle focus was never far away. In his mind, he was already imagining the fight and what he would do.

Suddenly, Senni looked at him with a serious expression. "Are we safe here? Do you think the Urghurs will come into the cave to get us?"

"Senni, we're working to make sure that doesn't happen."

"I'm frightened. Some of my friends said they eat little girls first."

"Don't listen to them. Stay with your parents and you'll be fine."

Senni smiled warmly and hugged Brady tightly. "I trust you."

It made him feel queasy. In truth, he couldn't guarantee the Urghur wouldn't win; her nightmare could come true. He didn't want to lie to her, but to speak the tenuous truth to her at that young age wasn't a good idea.

Brady returned her hug, kissing her on top of her head. Miran made it a group hug.

Sitting there, the family felt to him like his people. His affection for them was genuine. Beca was eyeing him longingly. He considered the matter. Was it so difficult a leap to take a wife? She was certainly appealing enough, and he truly cared about her.

Beca's mother spoke. "Girls, give Brady some space so he can breathe."

They released their grip, but still smiled at him.

"I like you," Senni whispered.

"I like you too, Senni."

They finished off the leisurely meal, then the group arose and went back outside the hut.

Beca and her father edged over to Brady. She remained silent while her father spoke.

"Brady, I've been teaching my wife to fight. She doesn't like it, but if it comes down to a battle right here in our city, I think we all must be ready."

"Hopefully, it won't come to that. We want to have that fight in their home, not ours."

"Can we do it, win this war?"

"I honestly don't know. It's going to be a bloodbath no matter where it occurs."

"We've wondered why such evil came to our world, if we did some great sin as a people to warrant this punishment."

"Sin has nothing to do with it. They're a predator species that happened upon your world, probably just by chance. This is what they do. They don't have remorse about harvesting the indigenous species on any of the worlds they invade. It seems to be their purpose, conquer and then devour."

"We're just food to them."

"There's no other way to sugarcoat the facts."

"As I think about it, this is probably why we've survived all of these ages. If the Urghur wiped us out, they lose their ongoing food source here. They wanted us to keep birthing new generations for them to cull. Finding us in our lairs wouldn't have been in their interests as long as they could continue to capture enough victims."

"It's a sobering fact, but there's no denying the truth of it."

"We thought we were so shrewd and clever, like we outwitted them. How naïve we were, basking in our false pride."

"Don't be so hard on yourselves. What's important is what happens now, going forward. At this point, looking back serves no purpose."

"What's that human saying? 'If you don't learn from your past, you're doomed to repeat it.'"

"That's true; it is one of our adages."

"Thank you for coming to spend this time with us, Brady. It's means a great deal to us."

"It means a great deal to me also. I haven't had a chance at peaceful family time in a very long time."

Chapter Nine

The fateful call came the following day from Colonel Severn.

"Brady, we've started the final push. The farthest Akara camps away from the suspected nest site are on the move. In each case, we've left enough troops back to protect the women and children, but we're moving at long last. There isn't any great strategy or tactic we can concoct. This will be getting down and dirty to slug it out, depending on our superior numbers to prevail. The Akara know this will involve high-casualty probabilities, but they also know holding back will lead to worse outcomes. Since you're much closer to the nest, your location will be one of the last to mobilize and move into position. Currently, we've got running battles going on with Urghur troops scattered across the planet."

"How are those battles going?"

"It's tough sledding, but the Akara forces are much improved. As I said, we use numbers to offset the Urghurs' physical strength. As we push them back and add more and more troops on our side in the push, the battles are getting to be more favorable for us. Moving forward, we're accumulating a formidable force. It's been good we haven't needed to provide air support to the ground battles thus far. If we can keep that up, we'll have air ordnance available for the attack on the main nest."

"I still wonder what surprises they may have in store for us."

"Likewise, but it's just something we have no control over. We adjust to whatever develops in the battle, like we always do. This time we do it without the corps and the fleet to bail us out."

"I've got to say, I'm proud of the Akara fighters. Against this scary foe, they stand in there and battle, no matter what."

"I agree. They've proven to be able allies and brave compatriots. Whatever happens in the end, I believe we will have done the utmost that could be done. I'll let you know later when to move your people into position, but you've probably got weeks, maybe as much as a month before the approaching wave gets to your location. In the meantime, if you want to organize your own local operations to bleed the Urghur, feel free. Every little bit helps."

"Keep me advised if they come up with some new tactic. I don't want any surprises."

"I will, Brady."

The city transformed when Brady sent out the word he had received from the headquarters. All of the hand-wringing contemplations were over. It was time to do what had to be done, regardless of the cost in lives. No one doubted that.

Rosca placed Brady in the position of commander over the Akara army, with Bralic as his second-in-command, the highest-ranking Akara soldier. Bralic had learned and adapted perfectly to the E3T ways, mannerisms, and levels of command competence. He was the perfect piece to fit into this puzzle. Brady had complete confidence in Bralic, as did the others of his team. That was significant, as this type of respect wasn't something members of the corps handed out easily.

Equally, Bralic ascended in the esteem of his people to a place rivaling Beca in notoriety and respect. With the advent of E3T communications in the world, this became a worldwide phenomenon where all the Akara citizenry worshipped the famous from afar, so to speak. Additionally, Beca was well aware of Bralic's fondness for her, and the fact the Akara people wouldn't have been unhappy if they became mates. However, she was focused elsewhere with her hopes in that area.

Meanwhile, the march toward the final battle continued, like their Armageddon was truly at hand. Brady monitored communications from the main base about the progress of the surge and ongoing battles elsewhere across the globe.

"So far, everything has gone as we expected," he explained to his closest people. Sara, Misty, Jocol, Bontag, Rosca, Bralic, Beca, and Visule were sitting with him, in addition to the senior officers of the city army.

"The Urghurs seem to have chosen to pull back rather than make any stands along the way. It looks like they're going to mass their forces around the main nest. They will bank on winning that fight, just like we will. I suspect they like their chances of getting all of us in the same place at the same time."

"How do we like our chances?" asked Visule.

"I wish I could say I'm confident of victory, but this will be a supreme test. If things were different, well, maybe I could be optimistic."

"You mean, if your fleet was still here, if we had adequate munitions, and if your full air force filled the skies."

"That is true. Those things would be a big help, but the reality is, we're going to take a hit in this kind of a fight. Even if we win, there will be considerable casualties."

They sat for a moment in grim silence, pondering the sad reality.

Rosca spoke. "Brady, I hope you know my people understand fully what must be done. There can be no retreat this time, and failure is not an option."

"Sadly, that's true, which is why we, as the leaders, must be quick to respond to shifts in the flow of the battle. If the Urghurs

137

have traps, secret strategies, and so forth, we need to have an answer before any of those tactics can turn the fight against us. I want to add, what air force we do have will refrain from blanket bombing. They'll overfly the battle site, but they must wait until we clearly identify the location of the nest before they jump into the fight."

"Which leaves the difficult work to the ground forces," said Bralic rhetorically.

"Correct. We have got to be relentless. I really hope their army is stocked with plenty of those immatures. If they've got reserves of fully grown, veteran, combat troops, our task becomes exponentially harder."

"We've had good success in clearing the local area around us," Bralic added. "Our tactic of going in overwhelming numbers is a good plan. I hope it's like a sample of what's ahead in the war. We do take casualties, but we win the fights in the end. However, as you said, we were facing less mature Urghur fighters. They seem to be in a delay mode to slow our advance toward their stronghold."

"I'm not surprised. I've always been curious at their command and control structure, if they have actual officers and leaders in our sense of it. With their hive-mind mentality, how they come up with ideas and strategies is a mystery to me. If they don't have particular key figures, it decreases their vulnerability. The queen seems to be their only indispensable individual at this point."

"I understand the army advance is probably less than two days away," said Beca. "Is there anything we need to do differently now in preparation?"

"Not really. We've made the assignments of who stays behind to defend the city. Other than that, we just assume our place in the noose that will be tightening on the Urghur troops."

"You said they see it as an advantage, us getting all of the Akara army in one place. I say it's an advantage for us," Rosca spoke.

The group gave an impromptu martial shout.

Smiling at the bravado, Brady continued, "I'd say we spend tonight with family. We can't know what our tomorrows will bring."

When the group broke up, Beca walked over. "Are you going to be joining 'family' too?"

He smiled. "Of course."

She smiled back in return.

Bralic eyed them thoughtfully and at length before he turned to walk away. Brady saw it and eyed Beca for her reaction. She seemed to be concentrating on not looking at Bralic, scowling away from eye-to-eye contact.

"Beca, you realize he is agog over you."

"I do."

"Does that mean anything to you?"

"You know my feelings, Brady."

"I'm just saying—"

"Don't bother, because I just might slug you if you do."

Brady laughed.

"You're very frustrating, Brady."

"I am that, Beca."

"What is it I must say, or do, to sink into your obstinate brain?"

"I don't have an answer for that question."

She stopped and turned to him. "Time is running out."

He paused. "Beca . . ."

Grimacing, she turned in anger and marched briskly away.

"Beca, wait." Trudging after her, his own confused emotions were stirred up.

Weather-wise, it was a miserable day outside. Gloom permeated the mood of the city residents, with the decrease in ambient light filtering in from the volcanic vent tubes. With volatile weather fronts normally fast appearing, the rainstorm on this day was a near deluge, pelting the ground outside so hard that the drops splashed up into the air. With a sustained weather front at such a level of ferocity, even the Akara pulled back their troops to positions of safety to wait out the lengthy inclement weather. The sound of the roar of the storm in the forest shaking the trees was so loud it could be heard in the city deep in the cave, further putting the residents on edge, like actual Armageddon was truly at hand.

Brady had every intention to follow Beca to join her family, but he paused a moment to ponder. She had a point that he needed to make a decision. Whether it was to marry her, or decline, she needed to be freed of the stalemate so she could move on, one way or another.

Mentally, he ran through the prime candidates once again: Sara, Misty, Beca, and Sonya; they were all compelling choices. About the thorny issue of making a choice in itself, had he decided to cross that threshold? Whether to pull the trigger was his first dilemma.

"I could die in this battle," he muttered, like it had never sunk in before.

As fast as the monster storm had rolled in, when it finally eased after an all-day pounding, it abated equally fast. The clouds dissipated quickly, and as sunlight brightened the sky, chasing away the gloom just before dusk, his spirits responded. Brady walked away, determined to finally break his personal stalemate at last.

When he got to the hut, Beca and her family had just come out as the illumination in the cave increased.

"Hello, folks," he said, plastering a smile on his face to Beca's glare.

Her parents smiled in return. Bren, her father, spoke, "Brady, you are welcome here. Thank you for coming."

"Can I borrow your daughter for a moment?"

Putting out his hand, Beca hesitated before accepting it. Brady pulled her around behind the hut to talk, out of sight of her family.

"I'm sorry to keep you hanging. I realize it isn't fair to you. You want a decision, so I'm going to do that. This is the most difficult decision I've ever had to make in my life. I like you all, so choosing one woman ... well, you can see how it had me stuck in neutral. You have abundant options, Beca. You already know that. I think there isn't an Akara male anywhere that doesn't want to be your mate."

Her eyes narrowed, like she anticipated bad news. He stopped for a moment, pondering again, *What was the best choice?*

"Just say it and get it over with," she huffed.

"Well . . . I don't understand why you, or any other woman for that matter, could find any semblance of merit in an old war dog like me, but . . . I guess if you want me, let's do this."

Anticipating the worst, she started to fume, but it dawned on her just before her angry outburst, he hadn't said no. It was far from the most romantic marriage proposal in history, but this was Brady, the soldier, after all. It was the best he could do.

"What?" she asked in confusion. "Are you saying . . . ?"

"I am."

Her total countenance changed completely. Rather than joy, she looked panicked. "I must . . . there is so much to do . . . a dress, I must get a dress. Brady, are you sure about this?"

"That is what I said. This could be the shortest marriage in history, but I'm on board with it if you are."

Suddenly, she grabbed him in a fierce hug. "I will be a good wife to you."

"I hope I don't disappoint you."

She grabbed his hand and dragged him back around the tent, where her family was waiting and watching expectantly.

"Mother, Brady has . . ." Beca was beaming.

Her family cried out in happiness before she could finish her sentence and rushed over to embrace them both. Bren shook Brady's hand.

"This is a proud moment in my family; our first daughter is about to wed."

"I'm sorry it's under these dire circumstances."

"It can't be helped. Get what happiness that you can."

"So, how do we handle this?"

"Our people have a ceremony, if you're agreeable?"

"I am."

"Brady, I must invite our friends," said Beca in excitement.

"Okay." Brady shrugged his shoulders.

Subsequently, it amazed him how fast everything came together in terms of organizing the ceremony, and the fact Beca had a white wedding dress magically appear, her mother's wedding dress. Brady was taking a wife on the same day as his proposal.

Later, when he put on his dress uniform for the occasion, he walked out to discover virtually the entire city was gathered to share the moment. It was a historic first for an Akara female to wed outside of the Akara people.

The Akara ceremony was shortened to satisfy human standards from the usual all-day ritual, and suddenly Brady had a wife. Sonya was flying back to headquarters at the time, but she radioed her congratulations. Sara and Misty were gracious. Jocol and Bontag were envious, though Jocol decided to attempt some humor after the women separated for their congratulations to the new bride.

"Brady, do you know what to do with her?" He laughed hilariously. Bontag joined him in laughing.

"Duh . . . very funny, guys."

"I was just checking."

"Your humor needs a lot of work, Jocol."

Rosca came over to join the guys. "Brady, we have your own separate hut ready for you to move into. I know this is a precarious time to start a new life with a wife, but I want to say on behalf of all the Akara people, congratulations, and more than that, thank you for showing respect and dignity to us. Placing us on a par with you and your people is very gratifying. I'm sure Beca will be a wonderful companion and mate."

"I have no doubts about that. I'm the one that's blessed that she would take me."

"We will give you all the time you desire under the circumstances. I think the advance of our army will arrive here within days, possibly a week at the most."

"I know. Thank you, Rosca. I want to go speak to Beca's parents, and then we'll start our brief honeymoon. As you say, there's no time to waste."

He plodded away, meandering through the heavy crowds, with well-wishers stopping him frequently. He could see Beca not far away, surrounded by giddy females, but he had to look to find Bren and Sala.

"Hi. Are you comfortable with me calling you Mom and Dad?"

"Of course," Bren replied. "It's . . . well . . . a little overwhelming having you enter our family, but a very good thing. With Beca and now you, the worldwide notoriety is unprecedented and, frankly, it's off-putting. We're simple people who now are seen as persons of significance. We've done nothing to warrant special attention from anybody."

"I understand those feelings. I've been deified to an extent, and I feel the same way. It's unwarranted, and I don't really like it. However, there's really no way to avoid the attention."

"The Akara have never been a society with stars, in your sense of the word. No one has sought individual acclaim before."

"Welcome to my world. I told you what we bring to the table can be good or bad. I wanted to say, I'll do my best to be a good husband to Beca. None of us can know what's going to happen in the war, but regardless, I'll do my best to be worthy of your incredible daughter."

"We know that, Brady," said Sala. "You realize all of the Akara women are envious of Beca."

Brady eyed her, curious at her playful smile. "Eh, thank you." It sounded more like a question than a statement.

With that, he turned to go over to claim his bride. She saw him coming and beamed a warm smile.

"Are you ready, Beca?"

"I am."

"Excuse us, ladies."

Taking her hand, he led her away, ignoring the avid stares and the murmurs of every female along the way.

"Are you happy about this, husband?"

He glanced at his wife. "What do you think?"

"I know how I feel, but I can only guess about you."

"No need to guess. Neither of us would be here if we weren't sure about getting married."

"I wish the Urghurs would just evaporate and be gone forever."

"Amen to that.

"Your worries about being distracted in battle, I've thought about that a great deal. I don't want to be the cause of it."

"Battle focus applies to both of us. You'll need to find it, also. You can't be out there worrying about me, and, certainly, you can't do something foolish that puts your unit at risk. If you're watching me in a fight, if I have a difficult moment, arbitrarily pulling out of a defense array makes that defensive alignment vulnerable. We don't need to talk about it right now. This precious time together is too valuable to waste. We worry about the tomorrows later."

"As you wish, Brady. I'm ready to be your wife in every way."

"Good, because I'm ready too."

"Does my appearance please you? Compared to your women . . . I must seem . . ."

"Beca, stop that. You're beyond beautiful. The fact virtually every male on this planet covets you should tell you something. As I told your father, I'm the lucky one in that you accepted me."

"Really, you think I'm beautiful?" She spoke with a sassy, provocative tone. Mimicking her human girlfriends, then she swished her bottom playfully as she'd seen human women do when they wanted to taunt males.

Brady chuckled. "Hubba hubba, baby. Come here, darling."

Their married life began. Brady experienced the feelings of love and adoration for the first time for his wife and from his wife. Being the center of another person's universe was very intoxicating, and coming to see Beca as the most precious living being in the world surprised him, a man who hadn't been emotional for much of his life as a bad ass.

They were slow to exit their hut the following day, as they were lost in the passions of young love. They were daunted by the stares of the people eyeing them like they were suddenly divine beings. Both merely nodded to the multitude of greetings from the well-wishers.

"Do you think this silliness from the people will ever end?" asked Beca.

"Well, I think the war will take care of that. Very soon, we'll all have our attention directed toward surviving."

"I hate the Urghur. I finally have the life I want, and now we must put our lives at risk because of them. It isn't fair."

"Life isn't fair, honey."

"I say this to you, husband. I will not waver out there in our duties. We will not allow these vermin to rule us with fear any longer. The Akara are not born to be food for vile creatures. We will prevail in the end, no matter what price we must pay."

Brady was moved by the strong emotions in her statement. He felt the same way. For possibly the first time in his military life, he had a just cause for going to war.

At a point in life where he should have been ecstatic with his new marriage, the threat of a quick end loomed like a vast phantom in the background behind them, swamping the happy glow of new love with the sobering reality of the approaching war. War he knew about very well. Soon, his bride would know more also, and that disturbed him greatly.

They spent as much time together as they could while working around their ongoing duties in preparation for the assault. In lieu of an actual honeymoon, a week was all they could salvage, as word of the first sightings of the approaching Akara massed armies spread quickly throughout the city.

Brady made one of his most difficult speeches ever when he talked to the Akara troops designated to stay behind to protect the civilians and the city. None wanted to be in that force, as they felt like they were shamed by being left behind. The final battle for the survival of all Akara was at hand, and they wanted to do their part.

"I understand your feelings, but your part is just as critical as anybody else's part. Our civilian populations are extremely vulnerable with the entire allied army on the move. If part of the Urghur plan is to raid civilian centers while the protection is reduced, it could be catastrophic. Do you see? If Urghur soldiers come here later, you will be the last line of defense for everybody's families. With no backup or reinforcements, your fight will be to the death, and that has to mean their deaths, not our women and children."

The grim-faced young Akara troops said nothing. Among them were the latest female training classes not far enough along yet to be ready for battles out in the field.

"You are the future. I can't guarantee what will happen in that fight at the nest. Perhaps the Urghur have other hidden bases and have new queens ready to step in if we take out this one. I'm sure the last thing on anybody's mind here is achieving glory and fame in battle out there or in here. To say this is deadly business is a colossal understatement. We all work together like cogs in a wheel to do our parts. Every cog is vitally important. We can't allow them to win anywhere."

These troops, virtually every one of them youthful, had none of the fear of their elders. They'd seen the Urghur soldiers being defeated, and regularly of late, so the prospect of battle didn't intimidate them. There was a singular look in their eyes, which heartened Brady, a look of steely eyed determination of purpose and the rejection of failure.

As he spoke, his wife stood by his side. Looking at her and seeing the abject adoration in her eyes, he was moved.

"I'm so proud of you, husband. There could be no finer man than you."

"I don't know about that, darling."

"I do."

"Let's . . ."

"Okay," she replied quickly.

They hustled away for some final brief moments together, driven to savor what little time they had left. The armies would arrive the following day, and they'd be obliged to join the surge and do their duties in the war.

The entire city was astir, as the sense in everybody was one of great foreboding. World war on this scale with the Urghur was all or nothing. Once the total Akara army was concentrated around the likely site of the main nest, there was no backing away to reconsider their choice. If the Urghur army had some surprise waiting, which would tip the scale adversely, the only choice of the allied army at that point would be to fight through it. That outcome was certainly no sure thing.

Trying to blot that troubling reality out of mind for one last night together, Brady and Beca concentrated on each other. The topic of the next day was purposely avoided.

That evening, city military forces congregated in deployment formations, since they had an early and prompt departure in the morning. Getting a good night of sleep was a challenge for everyone, as fear emotionally punished everybody.

Brady and Beca came out of their hut fairly early, when dawn's light was barely beginning. The scent of cook fires and early breakfast filled the air.

"Let's get plenty of food, honey. On these battle days, eating can be problematic. It may be a while until we get our next full meal."

Beca turned her head toward Brady as they walked. Speaking insightfully about the obvious, her sentences were rhetorical. "Are you still keeping my unit assigned to you in a support capacity? We can fight, Brady."

"I know you've been properly trained, and I don't doubt your abilities. We're going to drive forward, but in a cautious manner. I've got this feeling the Urghur troops have something ready to spring on us. I don't want to get sucked into some meat grinder situation, with no means of retreat, or with inadequate reinforcements to stem the tide."

"I see. I just didn't want to be held out of the fight. None of the women want that. We understand how deadly and dangerous this will be, but by adding our numbers, we may help turn a battle in our favor." Her tone spoke to Brady of her impatience with him.

"That's fine, but I'll make that decision. Echo Three Tango has been in the crucible so many times, honey. You develop a sense of the ebb and flow in combat."

"Okay, we will trust you, husband," she replied after a pause to consider his statement.

Walking over to the nearest serving center to get some breakfast, Beca heeded Brady's words and heaped plenty of food onto her plate. Spotting Misty and Sara sitting together, they went over to join them.

"Ladies," said Brady.

"Morning," they replied in unison.

Misty added, "Our scouts say the Urghur soldiers are starting to coalesce as we drive them backwards. The recent fights have been way too easy. They're clearly trying to draw us in."

"No doubt about it. I expected that. I wish I had some inkling of what they're plotting."

"Hi, Beca," said Sara.

"Hi."

"Don't let yourself get too stirred up. Once the fighting starts, things happen pretty fast, and mostly you react to changing battlefield issues."

"We will not disappoint you."

"That's not an issue, Beca. Your courage isn't in question. The female units will do us proud; I'm sure of it."

Beca smiled.

"Where are the guys?" asked Brady.

"They got an early start and went out with the pre-dawn patrols to assess Urghur movements."

Beca spoke. "I'm not afraid to join this battle, but I'll admit, I wish all of this was over and done."

"We all feel that. Now that you're married, you've had a taste of how life should be."

"Neither of you chose to wed?"

"It was tempting, but not at this time."

"I can tell you, marriage is all I hoped it would be."

All of the women looked mirthfully at Brady. He smiled sheepishly and shrugged his shoulders.

"You're very proud of yourself, sir," said Misty with a smirk.

"Well . . . yeah."

Everybody laughed.

"Good for you, Brady. Well done. You've made your new wife happy."

"I'm not trying to pretend I'm all that. Mostly, I got really lucky to have such a great wife as Beca."

She grinned warmly and then hugged him.

Chapter Ten

Brady walked out of the cave entrance with his wife at his side. The approaching allied army was very near at this point, and already the city army was pivoting to fill their place in the deployment array. They'd preceded the newlywed couple descending the mountainside to the base of the peaks to form up into battle formations.

The approach of the vast number of allied troops on the move was an inspiring sight. However, that fact still didn't offset Brady's concerns about the impending battle. The Urghur enemy had always proven to be stubborn fighters who took a serious toll in every battle. It never seemed to be in their playbook to back down.

Now, for the first time, he had a wife to worry about. Even trying to keep her nearby was no guarantee she would escape peril, or that he could feel she wouldn't suffer injury or death. It was disconcerting and had him off his game in terms of total battlefield focus. In battle, his emotions were not his friend.

Glancing at the ranks of the female Akara corps formed up in neat rows in perfect alignment, he could see they all had serious expressions, but they didn't show their fear. At this point, their initial number of fifty had greatly swelled with the addition of newly graduated classes from settlements around the planet, putting them into the thousands.

Regardless, Brady had no intention of throwing them into serious fights. Keeping them strictly as reinforcements went against what he'd told Beca, but Brady was fine with that. At least she might survive this by staying out of the frontline battles.

His old unit members meandered over to him, Sara, Misty, Jocol, and Bontag.

Misty smiled. "Here we go again. Are you ready for this, Brady?"

"I'm always ready."

"Really? Do you understand Beca can take care of herself?"

"I know that."

"Do you? I can tell by how you have them deployed you intend to keep them out of the battle. That will really anger them, and the battles may not allow you that luxury. It may take every single one of us once the shooting starts."

Brady turned his head. "Misty, I've got this."

She eyed him skeptically. "We'll see."

"I'm just being careful. These Urghur bastards are wily opponents. I've got this feeling we need to be very careful in what we do."

"Granted, but the women troops are part of our assets. You need to be able to use them."

"I am."

Now all of his E3T friends eyed him skeptically.

Ignoring them, he added, "Okay, guys, let's move out."

The inexorable tide of the allied army, fully united at last with the last pieces in place, rolled forward toward the unknown of this impending battle, the world war. Although Urghur soldiers were clear to see ahead, they continued to fall back, like they were taunting the allies to take foolish actions.

Meanwhile, the noose tightened around the supposedly hidden main nest. Many in the allied army were armed with Urghur weapons. However, a significant number of Akara warriors were still armed with primitive weapons.

All possible remnants of E3T survivors had been located worldwide and added to the attack force, numbering over eleven hundred. They were all armed with E3T weapons and were a potent force, and yet, even with those numbers, it was not enough to be a game changer.

The allied air force now consisted of four fighter squadrons. Uncovering more caches of ammo meant they could "bring the pain" far longer than anyone could have hoped for. They were supplemented by a number of drone aircraft. Although they had more drone aircraft available, the allies were limited by a lack of pilots to operate the unmanned craft. Training Akara soldiers to operate drones had been discussed, but it hadn't been a doable task in the short term.

The aircraft stayed back in the preliminary stages, waiting for the Urghur forces to make their move. Neither side fooled the other at that point. It would be a flat-out frontal assault.

Brady felt his usual adrenaline rush on the eve of battle. He'd been here too many times to be overcome with negative emotions. Ahead, they heard the sounds of the Urghur beginning their battle chants. For such a daunting sound as it had been to the Akara, now they responded with a vast chant of their own, filling the area with deafening sounds.

Behind him, Brady heard the female Akara corps adding their defiant voices in expressing their repressed rage against the vile Urghur scourge. He didn't dare look back at Beca, as losing his focus at this key moment was the worst thing he could do for him or for her.

At last, the Urghur horde started to form up and establish a skirmish line. They were not there in small numbers.

Brady muttered to Jocol, "I guess we can assume we're right about them having a new queen."

"Good, it's all the more for me to wipe out."

Brady smiled. "Be careful anyway. You might think you're invincible, but use your head."

"Always."

The Urghur chant rose as they built battle frenzy. The allies matched it with shouts and frenzy of their own.

It was an incredibly tense moment on the verge of the fight. Brady looked up and down the lines for any sign of Urghur traps. The allied army eased forward, gesturing and yelling, but they were still under control.

Arriving within weapons range of small arms, Brady raised a fist in the air for a pause before unleashing the attack. The allies roared and sprinted forward. The Urghur troops opened fire, but they maintained their positions in their defensive array.

At that moment, the allied aircraft swooped down to lace the Urghur lines with strafing runs, felling large numbers of the exposed enemy soldiers in a short amount of time. The Urghur troops suddenly dropped back into the nearby forest to resume a line of defense there where they were less visible to the aircraft. However, the air attack was so sudden that they incurred huge losses before they could race out of open ground.

Brady continued the charge, racing toward the Urghur front. As they reached the original Urghur line, he noted the considerable casualties from the aircraft runs, but they were too few for his liking. The Urghur soldiers were adjusting well to the allied battle tactics, and they remained a very daunting force.

As they approached the enemy troops, Brady's forces fired point-blank with E3T weapons, captured Urghur weapons, and primitive Akara weapons, felling numerous Urghur. The enemy soldiers remained fearless as ever, and returned fire, taking a toll among the approaching allies.

Brady could still hear the high-pitched screams of the enraged female corps directly behind him. They were not going to be content to watch the battle from afar. Akara casualties provoked them to feral action.

When they finally struck the enemy lines, as always, Jocol was unstoppable, scything his way into the midst of the enemy troops. However, he was one of a kind there. With all of the other impacts around him, going *mano e mano* was a different story. For the Akara, it was like hitting stone walls with the superior size and strength of the Urghur fighters. However, it helped a great deal that most of the enemy troops were the smaller, immature variety; the greater numbers of the Akara could have some success in overwhelming them. On both sides, there was considerable death.

Once they hit the line, Brady was immediately forced to concentrate on staying alive. Female Akara managed to drive ahead enough to be fighting at his sides. They were determined and driven, but in a smart way. Misty and Sara had been good teachers about the disparity of size and strength and how to cope with it. The Akara females never attacked alone and never exposed themselves to being overwhelmed in close-quarter fights.

As Brady fought, he switched to his right when he saw an Akara female suddenly alone and in trouble in the grasp of an enemy fighter. Brady killed the Urghur just as it was about to close its mandibles on her, and she jumped up without a pause to rejoin the fight. It inspired Brady that she could show such courage in the face of imminent death.

It was a fortunate outcome for that female, but Brady couldn't be everywhere to save other troops caught in Urghur grasp. He heard a scream to his left as a different female met her death in horrible fashion. It enraged the closest Akara males, who charged that Urghur soldier, slaying it in short order, and those directly around it.

Still, the battle soon became a quagmire, as neither side gained an edge. The allies were exacting a toll, but they were not able to break through the defensive line of the enemy.

As always, when an Urghur fell, its weapons were claimed by the allied troops and were immediately turned against the enemy.

Brady had no time to step back and ponder strategy. Every instant of time was a harrowing fight for survival.

Pounding at the line, Jocol felled any Urghur he could get near, and after a protracted time, he caused a bubble in their defensive array. The Urghur reinforcements moved to block his incursion before an allied breakthrough occurred.

Jocol seemed tireless, a titan, unstoppable and inexorable. Akara warriors surged to his sides to make a serious push into the enemy defensive array. In spite of the added Urghur numbers at the critical point, Jocol battered his way forward nonetheless. Massed Akara troops always attacked the Urghur soldiers in groups, so there were never any single-combat situations. It worked well, as this portion of the Urghur army was filled with younger, barely mature troops who were unable to have the successes of their older and experienced predecessors.

Gradually, the bulge in their line swelled further, and even the Urghur reinforcements couldn't stem the tide.

With a prodigious effort, Jocol burst through, opening a lane and establishing the first breach in the enemy lines. Urghur soldiers from both sides slid over to close off the breakthrough, but without success. When they moved out of position, it weakened the rest of the lines, and the allied troops there began to succeed in pushing back the remaining enemy troops.

The line started to bow badly, which inspired the allies to attack with a vengeance. With Jocol in the lead, they took advantage of the moment and gave the Urghur army a little of their own medicine by swarming and overwhelming enemy troops. Suddenly, it was the Urghur troops who were cut off and alone, facing swift death from the motivated allied fighters.

Brady caught a glimpse of his wife flashing past, leading a core of her sister fighters into savage combat. They showed no mercy and were daunting as they struck enemy Urghur warriors. Falling to the wrath of this newly elite female corps was a first. Seeing some of their sisters slaughtered in this battle had given the others feral hatred and the strong desire for revenge. These ladies were ready for war.

Even with this success, it remained a slow-going battle. The Urghur fell back, but they regrouped quickly, forming a new defensive line. The process started all over again. With the passage of time, abiding fatigue became a definite worry for the allies. Courage hadn't decreased, but overusing tired, rubbery muscles had an effect.

As a pre-arranged strategy, units were periodically pulled back for brief rests and to tend to wounds before moving back into the fight, which allowed other units a short respite. Fortunately, with the huge numbers in the allied army, it was a luxury they were able to maintain. It helped a great deal in coping with the fatigue.

In spite of this, on the other side, the Urghur never seemed to get fatigued. One could only kill them off to have hopes of ultimate victory.

Making slow but steady progress, the allied push kept buckling the Urghur lines, which occurred everywhere in the tightening circle. The circle around the site of the nest was enormous, so it took great effort to close in on their goal.

Misty and Sara tended to stay with the female Akara corps, joining their efforts to make a difference. Firing E3T weapons sparingly to conserve ammo, it wasn't an easy battle, even against

Urghur immatures. The ladies kept their heads, all working in groups when they attacked to guard each other and minimize further allied casualties in their unit.

Though they were doing well, the male Akara troops still kept an eye on them and were swift to intervene if any Urghur enemies started to gain an advantage.

The allied push meant they were going deeper into the forest and consequently were more obscured to the sight of aircraft overflights. There really was no way to get clean shots from the air, with both armies intertwined and no other path than slugging it out on the ground.

The Akara weren't losing, but they were enduring a terrible toll in lives in spite of the losses they inflicted on the enemy. No matter how many dead Urghur soldiers littered the field, there always seemed to be more pockets of resistance that popped up out of hiding. Even the wounded Urghur still posed a deadly threat, as they never backed down.

Brady glanced over as both Sara and Misty dragged Beca back. It was her turn for her unit to retreat for their rest, but she clearly didn't want to leave the fight. She looked at him before finally acceding. Misty and Sara stayed to rally the remaining troops in the continuing battle.

Jocol turned suddenly and drove to his left toward where the female Akara were engaged in a serious deadlock. Sweeping forward rapidly, he felled Urghur like wheat as he hit them from the side. It was a significant turn in the battle, as it allowed the Akara males to make a concerted push and cull the enemy troops at this point. Suddenly, the Urghur line collapsed, and they tried to pull back to reform, but Jocol and his mates wouldn't allow it. They'd seen this tactic in the daylong battle enough to be ready for it. Sensing this key moment, the allied reinforcements attacked in force to join the slaughter. Urghur reinforcements were blocked from rescuing their brethren, and in fact, they were battered backwards as the fight at this flashpoint started to become a rout.

The Akara army was relentless, mowing down any Urghur in their path. Urghur soldiers faced constant spear points, a barrage of arrows, and deadly Akara intent. This was in addition to the rapid uptick in newly armed Akara who wielded captured Urghur weapons. Brady felt some optimism at last as he raced ahead of his group just behind Jocol, who was trying to drive a wedge into the Urghur reinforcements so they couldn't form a new line.

Beca's rest was brief, as Brady saw her race back into the battle in a rush. She screamed her rage along with her sisters-in-arms as they struck the nearest Urghur soldiers. Again, they were too far away for him to be able to join in their fight. Brady had to concentrate on supporting Jocol, so he didn't get so far away that the Urghur could surround and cut him off from the allied army.

Wiping out the remainder of what had been the Urghur forces at this particular point in the line, the Akara soldiers raced forward, hitting the Urghur reinforcements before they were ready to make a stand. The battle seemed at a tipping point, as scrambling Urghur warriors were falling rapidly. The allies used so many newly captured weapons off the dead enemy soldiers against the Urghur that they continued to add muscle to the allied push.

Suddenly, the Urghur troops turned and raced back away from the allied assault. It was a first, as they'd never retreated in a battle. It struck Brady differently than he would have thought. Rather than rejoice in what seemed to be victory at this point, instead, his danger signals went off. Something didn't feel right about the Urghur retreat.

In the confusion and the din, he couldn't get the attention of the leading edge of the Akara assault line to slow them down. Rabid for victory and heedless of any hidden dangers, they raced in a frenzy after the Urghur troops.

Brady raced ahead at a sprint to grab Jocol and get his attention.

"Jocol, this isn't right. It feels like they're sucking us in."

Jocol blinked a moment, like he was just waking up. He turned and shouted in his deep, booming voice, "Stop, stop!"

The word started to spread throughout the attacking units; however, they were dispersed at that point, skewed out of proper alignment. They reacted too slowly to the risk.

It was at a place with concentrated undergrowth, which acted as cover, when suddenly, new Urghur warriors emerged. These mature warriors swarmed up out of the ground. Caught by surprise and out of position to use their tactics to outnumber the enemy, the lead Akara troops were caught in the trap and took serious casualties. The mature Urghur soldiers were especially vicious in how they slaughtered the hapless victims caught in the trap.

Gradually, Brady reformed his troops as quickly as he could, though too many were lost before they could move into the new fight in force. As they advanced, Akara soldiers raced back to escape the carnage of the ambush and into the safety of their approaching brethren.

Jocol took a deep breath, eyeing this serious challenge.

"Do you need to rest before we tackle this?"

"I can do this, Brady. We can't let them get any advantages. Literally chewing up those Akara was meant to intimidate and demoralize. We can't back down now."

"Okay, Jocol."

"Let's take it to those vile bastards."

Marching forward under better control, the battle resumed, but it was immediately a test for the allies, as across the front, these were no longer the immature. Success in the fight became exponentially more difficult. Akara numbers sufficed to keep the Urghur from gaining an upper hand, but at the same time, the allied push forward stalled.

Jocol waded into the nearest collection of the fiercest Urghur soldiers, and he was pressed to the limit to survive the encounter. These enemy troops fought differently by adopting the allies' strategy of watching each other. It was virtually impossible to isolate any of these enemy troops, and they were big enough to be nearly impossible to slay.

Akara hatred and ferocity had taken them a long way in the battle, but mostly, they'd conquered immature Urghur soldiers. Here, facing the power and ferocity of mature and fresh Urghur fighters, fatigue plagued the allies and blunted their attempts to press any initial advantage.

Calling a halt to the battle wasn't a viable option yet. Fighting all day with minimal rest and food was having a serious effect. If the allies pulled back, what the Urghur troops could accomplish in the meantime was a frightening prospect.

Brady debated in his mind what the best choice was, or even if there was a good choice. The strategy to bring the entire Akara army into this battle with their superior numbers was the only thing that allowed them to achieve a deadlock at this point, but only if they remained engaged in the fighting.

The new Urghur troops attacked aggressively, and although they could be killed, it was a far more difficult and costly task. Even Jocol hung back in a defensive posture as the battle assumed a position of stalemate. Brady worked his way over to Jocol.

"What do you think, big guy?"

"I think we must continue to fight, but I admit, we need to eat and to rest, if only briefly."

"My thoughts exactly. As much as I'm tempted to call in an air attack, I'm going to try to hold off because we need that air ordnance raining down on the nest."

"I can stand here if you want to pull back."

"Tell me the truth. If you're spent, say so. I need you at your optimum."

"I'll let you know when I can't continue. I need to be here against these fresh Urghur reinforcements. We can't have the Akara overwhelmed."

"Be very careful about engaging and getting cut off and surrounded."

"I will. You go and do what you must."

Reluctantly, Brady pulled out of the line and took some exhausted troops with him. Quickly sending word back to camp, food was sent for the frontline fighters as they moved back to rest. It was a continuous process, with the rest periods brief before the fighters returned to the lines to spell their spent comrades.

As Brady was returning to the battle, he looked over to see Beca coming out of battle and down the line for her rest period and food. She looked totally exhausted and had Urghur blood all over her. She also had Akara blood from slain comrades who'd been killed nearby enough to splash onto her.

He was moved to race over to comfort her, but he couldn't under these circumstances. Racing ahead, he forced a reluctant Jocol to back away and take his rest period, after which the Urghur made a fierce attack at the place where Jocol had been holding the point.

Brady assumed the point, and the Akara warriors surged to stand up to the withering assault. Losing momentum and suffering a break in the allied line wasn't acceptable.

Both sides incurred terrible losses of life. Each one of the Urghur matures they could kill was a great boon for the allies, as it was one less they had to continue fighting later. Behind these matures, their reinforcements were immature. Brady used it mentally as motivation to survive the tough fight. His mind reacted in his thoughts. *It gets easier if we can survive this.*

"C'mon men, we can win."

The Akara rallied and attacked in swarms to batter at the savage Urghur soldiers. It was as bloody a fight as Brady had ever been in, but it was still a stalemate. These daunting Urghur fighters were as savage and deadly as ever, and many Akara faced their end in horrible ways in the battle.

Brady killed the mature Urghur soldier directly in front of him, which caused a ripple in their line and caused the enemy reinforcements to move into action. Fortuitously, Jocol, reinvigorated after a short rest and food, appeared at Brady's side at that instant. He bashed down a mature Urghur to Brady's right and then another. When the enemy reinforcements plugged into the line, Jocol was ready, scything through them easily. The break in the Urghur line remained, and gradually it widened.

Pushing through the sudden gap, Akara troops were able to race through and get behind the Urghurs' skirmish lines. Turning and attacking the enemy from behind, the Urghur defenders caught in the vise now faced attack from the front and rear, and that spelled their doom. Making an all-out push, the allied army bashed the enemy troops down into the dirt, dead. It started a chain reaction, as troops were freed to continue racing behind the remainder of the Urghur lines, going both ways along the perimeter line. Urghur reinforcements were unable to stem the tide.

The battle had taken an unexpected and favorable turn. Brady was amazed to have this success against this enemy.

Turning to his left to race after his troops and toward the positions of the female Akara corps in the assault line, he assessed the situation on the run. Looking ahead, he could see Beca standing between Sara and Misty, and all were locked in combat, fighting fiercely against some mature Urghur soldiers. It was a serious fight, and the outcome was definitely in question.

Charging into the melee, Brady changed that dilemma as he and Jocol struck the Urghur soldiers from behind, quickly felling the dangerous knot of enemy troops and clearing his wife from that hazard in the process.

Beca looked at him, but it took a moment for her to focus and comprehend the changed situation. She was new to battle frenzy.

"Brady?" she whispered, like she was trying to make her brain function.

"It's me, Beca. Why don't you guys go back and rest."

"No, we had our rest and food. We need to press forward while we can. I don't think the Urghur fighters are done with this fight today."

"Okay, but I'm going to fight with you guys. Misty, have you seen Bontag?"

"The last I saw him was early in the morning. He was far down the line to our left. I haven't seen him since then. Jocol, it's good to have you here with us."

"I'm glad I survived too, and I'm very glad to see all of you. I always endeavor to stay above ground during battles."

Beca spoke with urgency. "Let's get back at it, husband. My people are still dying all around us."

"Sure, let's do it."

Racing down the line, the situation remained the same. The Urghur defenses were in shambles. For the first time, they were being battered back in a major fight and were actually retreating out of necessity.

It was so late in the day Brady hesitated to press the attack forward with the ambient light quickly fading. The planet's twin suns were barely above the distant horizon.

Sending out word, the allies called a halt to the fighting and formed up a defensive skirmish line of their own. The dead allied troops were hauled away, the wounded sent back for treatment, and food continued to be brought down to feed the troops at the assigned positions in the lines. It was a much-needed respite for the exhausted fighters. Fortunately, the Urghur army made no late moves in the dark to try to take advantage of the lull.

Brady hurried to locate Bontag, who had been nicked up and was receiving medical treatment with the E3T miracle potion; he was healed in short order.

"Bontag, it's so good to see you," said Misty, moving in for a warm hug.

"Thank you. It was perhaps the most difficult battle I've ever been in. I had so many close calls, I lost track. It was a miracle that I survived, although I need to give the credit to the bravery of the Akara troops rather than just pure luck. They protected me, sacrificing their lives to do it. I'm grateful, but I'm greatly saddened by the loss of so many great souls. They deserve to live as much as I."

"I know, Bontag. We knew it would be terrible, but a person is never really ready for the horror of enduring it."

Bontag turned his head to Brady. "I didn't think we would win, even with them reduced and weakened."

"I think we all were worried. At this point, I'm grateful to still be standing, but I worry about tomorrow. The enemy adapts from their experiences, so if that means a change in their tactics tomorrow, we need to be just as adaptable."

"It would be so nice to be able to call down the fleet to wipe out these bastards."

"I know, Bontag."

Brady put an arm around his wife, who was sitting in silence. The stress of the day, the fear about being killed still seemed to haunt her, along with the continuing pain of seeing her comrades slain.

"Beca," he whispered.

"It was horrible, but I will endure it," she replied softly. "It's the same for all of us, my Akara brothers and sisters. This loss of precious life is unbearable, but there is no other way."

She looked all the more forlorn as the skies had changed to gloomy with a fast-approaching weather front. Quickly, rain drenched them and continued all night long.

Brady kissed the top of her head and squeezed her gently to provide some emotional comfort. She returned his hug.

"*Deus auxilium nos,*" Brady whispered.

"What does that mean?"

"God help us."

She repeated the foreign words softly, "Deus auxilium nos."

The couple remained silent and intertwined for a time before she spoke again, pulling back to look in his face. "I don't know how you humans endure this. What we're forced to do, it's . . ."

"Savage, brutal, bestial? There was no way I could explain it beforehand so you'd understand, honey. It's why we were all hesitant about taking a mate."

"I wonder, if we survive, will this warp us into dark creatures we don't wish to be?"

"I can't tell you there are no lasting consequences to fighting and killing, but we can survive it, and we do. Acknowledging our inner darkness, it's a part of us we can never fully forget, but with time, we cope and do find ways to deal with it. It's still a test for your feelings, though, there's no way around that."

Brady noticed all the silent faces around him, including his four E3T mates, who listened to his explanations. They also looked forlorn, wrapped up in their ponchos.

No one said anything as they dealt with their own inner demons. None of them failed to understand Brady's words.

There was nothing happening on this battlefield, or any other, that a person could point to with pride. Survival was intertwined with slaughter. Though his words were true, it wasn't an emotional fact that could be discounted or dismissed. Coping wasn't such an easy task, and the Akara had far less experience with it than war veterans like E3T.

After concluding his remarks, Brady embraced his wife in a firm hug. Beca remained hollow-eyed with a haunted expression on her face.

"I understood you, Brady, what you told us about battle, but you're right that no words could fully prepare us. It was ... horrible. I was terrified from start to finish. All that I could do was react to threats from moment to moment all around me. Is this how your life has been?"

"Yes. Regretfully, that's true. The difference for us is the Akara are fighting in a noble attempt to survive and throw off the tyranny of brutal overlords. Our battles in the past have been far less noble as we followed the orders of superiors with impure motives of conquering for greed. I've felt ashamed numerous times about our assignments and our actions."

"I'm so sorry. I wonder if there is an ultimate reckoning for those types of people for the wrongs they do."

"I'd like to think so, but honestly, their power, money, and influence have always insulated them from any consequences. It's a crime of epic proportions, but we in the army can do nothing about it. We're just expendable grunts."

Beca was silent, pondering the noisome situation.

"It's funny when I think about the actions and motives of the Urghur. In a way, they're possibly better than the E3T leadership. At least with the Urghur, their purpose of hunting for food sources makes sense, although the motives are dark ones for the victims. With us, much of what we do is so needless."

"Let's not talk any further. It's too depressing."

"Sure."

Chapter Eleven

Morning came too soon for the allies, who were still exhausted from the prior all-day battle. Fortunately, the Urghur army had made no probes or incursions during the night. Still, it was a fitful time, trying to get restful sleep while worrying about a possible attack. Memories of the horrors of battle weren't easily purged from the mind, nor were the turbulent emotions easily calmed.

It was another dismal day with rain falling from an overcast sky. The weather front remained for the entire day, and the pounding rain made the footing slippery.

Even with the Akara cleats on their shoes, it required greater care for allied soldiers to move about.

The enemy were assembled and deployed in multi-tiered skirmish lines. The huge numbers of their losses seemed to have been absorbed with no problem and were replaced by those numbers. It was a chilling thought that the new queen could pump out hatchlings at such an astounding rate.

The allies were not quick to return to battle; they took their time to eat breakfast, to rest further, and to gather their wits. The prior day, too many allied soldiers killed in battle had been dragged away to be food for the Urghur horde, this in spite of a conscious attempt to deny the Urghur soldiers their ghoulish food source.

Behind Brady and Beca, the female Akara corps was sitting in a tight conclave, sharing their troubled feelings. Their courage hadn't evaporated, but the horror of this war had a strong effect. After all, it was their first meaningful, full-fledged battle.

Beca looked back at her sisters-in-arms. Uniformly, she saw the same haunted expressions.

"Brady, will we be warped forever by this, if we survive?"

"I'd say different individuals react in different ways. Some will cope better than others. Some may not cope at all. I've seen some tragic endings for soldiers who suddenly lost it and went off the deep end."

Beca shuddered. "I wonder if I will become one of those unfortunates?"

"We've got each other. I'm right here for you, honey. What we're forced to do isn't something we're designed for, this taking of lives. It isn't our normal state, being killers."

"I'm sorry; I must sound so weak. You deserve better in your mate."

"Don't be silly. You're doing just fine."

"I wish this nightmare was over."

"I feel that sentiment frequently."

Jocol ambled over and stared at the huddled group.

"I know; we've got to get going," Brady muttered. He stood up, along with Beca. The female corps stood up immediately, the hard looks back in their eyes.

"Let's do this thing." Brady saw allied troops rising up all the way down the lines in both directions. It was time to resume their deadly business.

Brady remembered his own training days from long ago and the instruction of his mentor; *survive and advance* came to mind. Brady wasn't sure who in history first made that prophetic adage, but it was true for any war anywhere.

Sloshing ahead through puddles in the storm, they approached the enemy troops. The Urghur made no moves to come out at the allies. Also, they didn't make any of their usual terrifying sounds, which was a clear departure from their norm. It was worrisome for Brady. However, there was no other choice but to engage them where they stood.

Nearing the skirmish line, they could hear the start of battle farther down the lines in both directions. Brady raised his fist to signal the start of hostilities. They charged suddenly across the short distance to close on the enemy soldiers, and it was fierce fighting from the start. The seemingly tireless Urghur posed as difficult a challenge as ever.

The script was the same as the prior day, slugging it out for mere feet of ground. Culling the Urghur horde was as daunting a task as the prior day, and again allied dead and wounded were dragged away by Urghur units assigned to that task.

Brady felt helpless, lacking any strategy he could enact to halt those vile Urghur actions.

On this day, Beca honored his request to stay nearby him. The female corps formed up and deployed around Brady and pushed ahead directly behind Jocol's savage attack.

Again, after considerable fighting, Jocol managed to bash through the initial skirmish line and then batter through the next reserve line and then the next.

This time, rather than allow the allied troops to get behind Urghur lines, they suddenly pulled back to redeploy.

It was an incremental success, if taking ground was the goal. However, felling Urghur troops was the real goal they needed. It was discouraging how they always seamlessly replaced their numbers, so it was hard to envision any realistic end in sight.

Hour after hour of intense battle passed by with the same, slow progress.

Jocol was suddenly beset upon by four huge Urghur troops who tried to pull him down. Brady reacted immediately. His

E3T mates were nearby to help protect their greatest fighter. Misty, Sara, and Bontag used their E3T weapons to mow down the attackers, but the Urghur continued a determined assault, like they sensed the E3T were the key to winning the battle and the war.

Jocol fought like a berserker, but these were experienced, mature Urghur soldiers attacking him in numbers. Brady managed to fight to his side to help with the onslaught. He could hear the sound of E3T weapons as Urghur fell all around him.

Suddenly, Beca was beside Brady, fighting desperately. This close quarter, hand-to-hand fighting was the very thing Brady had warned the females to avoid. However, more Akara females joined the fray, pushing ahead to use their strategy of superior numbers to overcome the enemy troops. They were not going to lose their leaders.

Brady changed his fighting tactics to protect his wife. It was the very thing he'd worried about.

Beca shouted to him. "Do not do this!"

She attacked an Urghur soldier with a group of her sisters. Brady returned to protecting Jocol's back.

Keeping Jocol alive was an accomplishment, yet the battle was a stalemate. Again, for as many enemy troops as they brought down, there seemed to be an endless supply of reinforcements to step into any breach.

Misty was knocked backwards and into Brady's arms by a huge Urghur mature. They both attacked it with a vengeance. Even with both of them, it was a serious and protracted fight, which only ended when Misty fired her E3T weapon point blank into its face.

"Thanks, Brady."

"You're welcome."

He glanced back to see Beca and her mates had brought down their big opponent. Quickly moving on to another enemy soldier, they were relentless.

Jocol's fight reached the tipping point as he felled the last of the big matures near to him, and suddenly they were able to drive forward again. Again, the Urghur soldiers suddenly retreated to reform their lines.

As with the prior day, it was tiring duty, and with the passage of time, exhaustion took a toll, even with the allied strategy of alternating troops for rest and food. Brady struggled to fight through the physical and mental fatigue. He was not alone in that state.

The Urghur horde remained a stubborn foe, unwilling to concede defeat. In fact, they were the most intractable foe Brady had ever faced on any planet, and he found trying to be optimistic was difficult. He mirrored Beca's wish that the battle was over.

Still, the female Akara corps fought bravely, never backing down from their opponents. Although they suffered casualties, none shied away from any fight. This further inspired their male counterparts to their utmost effort.

Meanwhile, the Urghur enemy never changed in their approach and in the severity of their hazard. If any Akara made even the slightest error of judgment, horrible death was swift to follow, usually in the large mandibles of the enemy troops.

When this day of battle wound down at dusk, the progress of the allied drive seemed minimal. The Urghur now pulled back their own dead as they retreated, since the allies refused them the opportunity to drag away any allied dead.

"My guess is food is getting short for them, so apparently cannibalism isn't an issue," Bontag commented.

"That wouldn't surprise me," Sara replied.

"They have no honor," Beca remarked.

Brady opined, "I think they're such a radically different species, they legitimately do not look at things like the rest of us. Showing insect or reptilian behaviors rather than any actions of higher or advanced species, in my opinion, accounts for these radical differences we see. Perhaps we've been judging them wrong all along. If they operate like a swarm of bees or ants, for example, their thought patterns may be elemental or instinctive."

Misty replied, "That wouldn't explain their technology. They have modern weapons; they have space travel, surface flying craft. A bunch of insects didn't sit around and dream that up."

"True. It's difficult to put those two aspects together."

Jocol piped in, "Perhaps they conquered a higher race and basically stole the advanced weaponry we see?"

"I wonder . . ." Brady answered thoughtfully. "I wondered why these particular Urghur soldiers are suddenly cut off here. Our fleet is gone by choice, but in their case, perhaps there are technical difficulties."

"Interesting theory," said Sara.

"If they're using stolen technology and equipment, they may have no way to repair, refit, and/or adapt to normal battlefield losses or routine maintenance issues. Perhaps their supplies of fuel and ammo are finite also."

"That would be a very good thing," Misty remarked. "It would mean if we can wipe out these bastards here and now the problem is solved once and for all."

"Exactly. If it's true they're an opportunist, predatory species living off others, it would explain a great deal in the seemingly inexplicable task of understanding their motives and strategies. They're definitely unlike any opponent we've ever faced."

Misty muttered, "It's a painful test so many of us must die to end the occupation."

Nobody replied to the obvious statement. They all knew it was an expression of emotion and grief rather than a restatement of facts.

"*Carpe diem,*" said Brady. He hadn't intended it as a joke; however, his mates chuckled.

Beca eyed them curiously. "What? What does that mean?"

"Seize the day," Misty explained. "It means Brady is a total jarhead, lacking a brain."

Brady smiled at her and then at his wife.

"I don't understand, husband."

"Good. If you understand our banter, it would give you a nosebleed, and you'd probably need therapy."

His four partners all laughed heartily. Beca had a puzzled expression. "I don't always understand your jokes."

"Don't worry about it. It doesn't take much to entertain us in the corps. If we ever start to make sense to you, that's when you have a problem."

"Oh." Her puzzlement continued. "I . . . eh . . ."

"Beca, it's not important. Put it out of your mind."

"Okay. I'll try. I still want to 'get a handle' on human humor, to use your words."

"A noble goal, honey."

"That's more humor."

"It is, but at a feeble level."

At that moment, the Urghur soldiers started their war chants, like a signal for the allies to answer the challenge. As many times as Brady had heard that sound, it continued to be chilling. He felt an element of mental fatigue as he tried to gather his wits for what was coming.

"Let's hit it, folks."

Up and down the allied lines, troops started to inch forward. The size of the ring of allied soldiers tightening on the Urghur nest was still a considerable circumference. Ahead, there was no sight of their ultimate goal, the nest itself.

During this phase of the ground war, the allied aircraft remained at their air base. They were preserving ordnance for the final assault, and it served no purpose to waste fuel on mere overflights. There was nothing to be gained. The Urghur army was right there in front of the allies.

Brady gave his wife a hug before he started moving forward. The female corps was close behind him in a tight configuration. Jocol was at the point again, with Bontag, Misty, and Sara walking side by side.

On this day, just before getting within striking distance of the Urghur lines, Brady ordered rank after rank of Akara troops, who were lined up behind the entire allied advance, to use bows to launch waves of arrows at the Urghur troops. It was a variation from any prior allied tactic, and it caught the Urghur troops by surprise. That barrage continued until the Urghur fighters reacted by trying to protect themselves from being punctured.

At that instant, when they were distracted, Brady ordered the charge. The allied soldiers screamed their challenge and raced toward the Urghur troops, who were scrambling back to reform the skirmish line.

The impact with untold collisions everywhere along the lengthy front was a huge sound. Many lives were lost in mere minutes, but fortunately a lot of those lives were Urghur.

This time, with Jocol leading the way, Brady's forces quickly punched a hole in the enemy line, and soon there were allied troops in the open behind the Urghur. Again, they went down the lines in both directions, attacking the enemy from the front and rear simultaneously.

The battle was off to a fortuitous start. Brady didn't notice any preponderance of the large, mature Urghur soldiers. Immature opponents were coming to be the norm as the days of fighting went on.

Pushing ahead, they gained more ground than nearly all of the prior days combined. Going into the heavier forested areas, the fight was virtually obscured from surveillance from above. The allied aircraft remained grounded.

Jocol was a beast in the fighting, felling large numbers of enemy troops and leaving a trail of enemy bodies behind him. With his E3T partners deployed around him in a normal corps array, protecting all sides, they were virtually invincible. Beca and her Akara female corps members stayed close behind the E3T soldiers. They kept the Urghur from flowing in behind E3T to cut them off and surround them.

The fighting came to a standstill for a considerable time as neither side could gain an edge. As always, it was a bloodletting with substantial casualties on both sides. This time, however, the allies made a concerted effort to deny the Urghur troops the chance to haul away those casualties, whether Akara or Urghur, and have them become their daily food.

On this day, Brady noted the minimal number of the experienced, mature Urghur. Regardless of the adverse turns for the enemy, Brady took it to mean the remaining crack troops were held back elsewhere, probably for defense of the queen. The smaller, younger troops fought diligently, but the task for Brady's army was marginally easier.

As always, Jocol was a titan, bashing away any and all impediments in his path as he wouldn't allow the Urghur to regroup and reform their skirmish line. Brady worried, though, that as they continued to move deeper into heavy woods he didn't know what was happening to his sides, as he couldn't see very far. Each foot of ground they gained here moved them even deeper into heavy concealment, and the feeling of battlefield isolation increased.

Toward dusk, their progress forward slowed as they reached a point where the ground started an ascent up a huge hill.

Brady called a halt to the attack and eased his troops back enough to break off the fighting. The Urghur remained very near to the allied line and switched their tactics, rushing forward to try to claim as many of the dead as possible. The allies went into a defensive mode, firing weapons constantly to deny the Urghur their noisome, ghoulish goal. It ended up being virtually a series of chess moves all night, which meant allied troops had to rotate sleep in increments to leave enough fighters on the line to continue the fight. It was fatiguing and difficult in the darkness.

Brady had to order Jocol to stand down, as he was the one key allied soldier who had to be rested for each new day. It was an imperative Jocol didn't like, and he only grudgingly acceded to Brady's command.

"Listen, we need you fresh every day. There will be plenty of them to deal with tomorrow."

Jocol shrugged before turning away. "I don't like these brave Akara being killed."

"None of us do."

The Akara female corps deployed and ringed in a protective circle around Jocol when he lay down to sleep; they did the same around Brady. Beca lay close beside her husband. Meanwhile, the nocturnal skirmishes continued through the rising of the sun the next morning.

After a quick breakfast, Jocol attacked the nearby Urghur with a vengeance. Their mixture of troops with very few of the mature soldiers remained the same, and again allied progress forward was good. Fighting their way up a hill wasn't easy, but that was the task at hand. The Akara didn't complain. They simply set about doing what needed to be done.

Brady felt as proud of these noble people as fellow fighters as he had about any comrades in his life. These weren't warlike, trained killers going about the butchery of war, absorbing casualties of friends and family. They were decent individuals, moms and dads, sacrificing their lives to prevail on behalf of their people.

It inspired Brady, and it was obvious it motivated Jocol. On this day, he was driven to killing off Urghur soldiers at an even higher rate.

Jocol's success forced the Urghur to rotate troops down the line from each direction to compensate for their losses at his hands as their reinforcement reserves were already drawn into the defensive fight. It meant their entire line gradually weakened, allowing the allied army to take the advantage.

Surprisingly, it was a single combat, Jocol engaging a huge Urghur, that took on great import in the battle and the war. The giant Urghur was the field leader of the enemy troops, and it was a savage fight. As difficult as it was for Jocol, who was fighting up a steep section of the hill, he would not relent bashing at the giant creature. The whole battle swayed back and forth, as if both sides were dependent on the outcome of Jocol's death fight.

This enemy soldier was experienced and posed a terrible challenge for the allies' champion. For the first time, Brady was worried as he concentrated on protecting Jocol's back from Urghur attempts to aid their own leader.

The overall battle hung in the balance, seemingly for an eternity, as the two larger-than-life titans exchanged massive blows at such a rate they looked like blurs. The difference appeared to be that Jocol's emotions were driving him to his utmost effort. He was not going to let the Akara perish, if he could help it.

The Urghur leader was like a single spear point for their side, sharing the consciousness and thoughts of the whole, and that included the queen, hidden in her lair. It fought with equal battle fervor, as for them, this was their survival too.

It was a different dynamic, as both sides realized the end could hinge on this outcome.

Suddenly, the Urghur champion exercised a feint and tried for a killing blow in close quarters to exploit a small advantage. Through his fatigue, Jocol was not quite fast enough to fully elude the swipe, and he was nicked by the glancing blow, which knocked him off balance. As he was falling backwards, the Urghur monster pounced, trying to make the kill.

Brady reacted in an instant, drawing his sidearm and blasting the Urghur point blank. At the same time, Jocol only seemed vulnerable, reacting also as the Urghur closed on him, opening its own vulnerability. He pivoted and slammed a fist into the throat of the monster, brought up a knee into a savage smash into its abdomen, and then grasped its head in both hands to snap its neck in a quick, wrenching move.

The most daunting individual Urghur fighter was slain, and the entire battlefield reacted. The Urghur suddenly paused for a moment in stunned silence and then retreated quickly.

They heard cheers along the entire line from the allied army before they raced ahead to press the advantage before the Urghur troops could regroup.

Cresting the top of the hill, at last they had arrived, with their goal in sight. The remaining Urghur army was massed in a final defensive array. The nest entrance seemingly was in the center of their deployment.

Urghur troops were flooding into the gaps until they were a solid line, shoulder to shoulder. Here came the last defenders, the protectors of the queen, and they were large.

Allied troops surged forward on all sides as the noose was tightened.

Brady got on his radio to call in the air force. In mere moments, their surface craft swooped in, guided by handheld lasers from the E3T ground troops, since their sight lines were obscured by the heavy forest at that point.

It was like a mini-apocalypse, as foliage and Urghur exploded everywhere in an eruption of concentrated allied air firepower that joined the ground fire. The allied army waited for the aircraft to cull the enemy army as much as could be done. The Urghur soldiers tried to scramble underground, deep into the nest to avoid death, but the directed allied air assault followed them down the tunnel with precision-guided firing. The resulting concussions shook the ground under the allied feet and were so powerful it was difficult to keep from falling over.

The aircraft pulled back while Brady ordered another ground attack. Racing ahead in a fierce headlong sprint, Jocol was the first to rush down into the nest. The air attack had felled huge numbers of Urghur, but as they moved deep underground, they hadn't been able to penetrate down to the queen or the hatchery.

Here, the remaining Urghur troops made their stand. For both sides, it was do or die. Allied troops surged into the cavern behind Jocol. The Urghur troops were loud with their battle frenzy.

For the first time, the allied troops got a glimpse of the queen. Although a female, she was huge, much larger than the biggest of her soldiers. She had greater reach than any of her soldiers and was incredibly nimble, despite her size. Her mandibles looked large enough to consume multiple opponents simultaneously.

What remained of the mature and elite Urghur fighters were poised around her.

The fight was vicious from the start, and in this confined area, there was no retreat. The allied soldiers continued to flood down the tunnel, intent on wiping out this disgusting threat once and for all. Pressing forward in a mass, they meted out death against even the best of the Urghur soldiers. It was primal savagery taken to the ultimate—kill or be killed.

There was no other option than this protracted, vicious fight. Killing any Urghur soldier left one less to confront them. However, it was still a battle that claimed too many brave Akara lives.

Jocol avoided a sudden attack by four massive Urghur soldiers. They knew he was the lynchpin of the allied army and tried to take him down. They failed. Brady, Bontag, Misty, and Sara fired E3T weapons point blank, as did the Akara, firing captured Urghur weapons to slaughter these dangerous enemy defenders. An Akara, the first allied fighter to break through the defense ring and approach the queen, met a terrible end, as she was a physical force capable of defending herself. With her great size, she wasn't a good candidate for one-on-one combat. She snapped up the Akara, popping him into her mouth with a sickening crunch, then closed her mandibles and swallowed him whole.

That incensed the allies, and Jocol in particular. He battled his way ahead, fighting off Urghur attacks to lead a group approaching the queen. She snarled her challenge, and suddenly the remaining Urghurs drew back to present a tight ring around her.

It was the worst battle Brady had ever experienced. The queen could reach over the tight skirmish line in any direction to skewer allied troops, lifting them bodily before popping them in her mouth. Killing the Urghur troops was incredibly difficult, as they fought like berserkers, and they were shoulder-to-shoulder, so they could work in conjunction to protect each other. Jocol was the only allied soldier to have any level of success.

Trying to slay these defenders with swords and spears was impossibly difficult. Emptying their remaining modern ammo into the line left them with no other choice but to battle with primitive weapons. Already, Akara archers had pelted the queen, who had numerous arrows sticking out of her, but she seemed unfazed. Whatever injuries those arrows caused didn't seem to weaken her.

The queen was a savage opponent, meting out death easily. Her tight knot of defenders stood together, impenetrable and invincible, as she bellowed deafening shrieks and roars. It was a single-minded, last-ditch stand, with no retreat possible for either side, but suddenly she paused, immobile, and went into a momentary trance.

After this moment, the queen let out a loud, wailing sound. Allied troops elsewhere had reached the hatchery and regretfully had started to butcher the hatchlings and their guards. It was a horrible task, but a necessity. The Urghur could not be allowed to continue to propagate and resume their threat.

Vicious and incensed, the queen reared up and reached for Jocol, her most fearsome opponent. He ducked and rolled under her first swipe, springing back up to swing a sword to lop off a portion of her nearest joint. She screamed in pain, but she redoubled her efforts to kill.

The E3T soldiers moved to the front of the whole ring around the queen. They were bigger and stronger than any Akara fighter.

Rosca had ceded those key positions and had his fighters in close support, firing continuous arrows and throwing spears into the remaining Urghur fighters.

The queen had so many arrows stuck into her at that point, there was nearly no other place they could pelt her, yet her level of fighting was unchanged.

She was concentrated still on trying to get at Jocol, and she suddenly made a desperation move, lunging toward him, leaping over her ring of defenders.

Jocol scrambled backwards, rolling again to avoid her stabbing attempts to skewer him.

The few remaining weapons with any ammo were emptied into her at that point; however, she still moved ahead, chasing after Jocol.

He made his own sudden move, turning and then diving under her massive body to strike upwards. She cried out at the wounds he inflicted, but she remained in the fight, managing a wound of her own with a swipe of her talons across his back as he rolled to get out of her reach.

Jocol yelled at the pain. The E3T troops attacked her to defend their comrade, and she reacted violently. Brady took a blow to the head from a backhanded swipe, but fortunately, he was not sliced by her talons.

Jocol got up to engage a huge Urghur soldier charging to try to kill him. A steady barrage of Akara arrows slowed that trooper, allowing Jocol to put an end to his threat.

Brady rejoined the mass attack on the queen. She fought for her life against increasingly difficult odds as her few remaining troops fell all around her.

When they were all gone and only she remained, she let out a bone-chilling shriek and made a final attack to take out as many allied troops as she could. However, there were too many of those troops, and they would not be denied.

At long last, the queen was hacked down to the ground and slain. The Urghur occupation of the Akara planet had ended in brutal fashion.

Rather than cheering in celebration, the whole allied army collapsed in exhaustion and looked around at the terrible carnage and the considerable loss of life. Rosca came over to sit down beside Beca and her female warrior friends. It was a heartrending scene as, for the first time, they experienced the feelings of loss. Being alive, surviving the terrible battle came with a heavy price, and they all felt pervasive guilt when so many others had perished. Fathers, sons, wives, and daughters, it hadn't mattered. No one was spared loss in their families.

Brady walked over and heard Beca ask, "Why are we alive when so many others are not? We're no more deserving of life than any of them who died."

"I understand what you're feeling, honey. Every soldier faces what is called 'survivor's remorse.'" Brady then hugged her. He knew the feeling all too well.

Chapter Twelve

"We did it," Brady muttered to Rosca as they gathered later to assess the scene.

"I'm being honest with you, I didn't think we could prevail. I only hoped we could." Rosca's voice shook, as he was in shock.

"We did it," Brady replied again, muttering in a softer, contemplative voice as he looked again at the bodies of the fallen.

Suddenly, Beca pulled her hand from his back and looked at Brady's bloody wounds with concern. "You're injured."

"We all got nicked up, honey."

"We need to address your wound so it doesn't fester."

They looked around for the healers, who were busily moving about the numerous injured troops. Jocol was lying on his stomach while they stitched up the deep lacerations on his back.

A young female came over after noticing Beca's glance. "I will help you."

Brady's cuts required stitches also, in multiple places.

Beca sat holding his hand.

He turned his head to her. "It's a good thing the Urghur talons weren't poisoned. We've fought against creatures on other planets in the past where you couldn't allow them to cut you."

"It's hard to get my head around the fact that they're gone. They've been here for so long a time. Generations have lived and died for ages under their dark menace."

"Life can get better now."

She replied, but it sounded more like a question. "Yes."

The E3T corpsmen, in agreement with the Akara general staff, left the Urghur dead bodies piled in the cavern. They placed considerable explosive charges, then they buried those remains by collapsing the hill down upon them.

The allied troops remained for an entire day at the site of the final battle to perform a solemn Akara religious rite as a tribute and eulogy to the legions of allied fallen; Brady and his mates were moved. The finality of closure after battle wasn't a luxury they ever received in their endless duties in the corps. E3T dead were expendable and acceptable components of war to the high command and their bosses.

Brady stood with his E3T comrades and muttered, "It seems the point of view of Corps Command is, if they allow the troops to contemplate, it might lead to consequences, and consequences aren't allowed in the corps. There could be bad ramifications for the select, the power brokers at the top. This service was a nice gesture. We should have been allowed to do it all along."

The following morning, the army dispersed, heading back to their homes. Now they could move out of the caves and take up residence on the surface on the open ground of their own world. The remnants at the sites of ancient Akara cities had eroded and crumbled to the ground, because so much time had passed in hiding below the surface.

Beca walked beside Brady. "I've never lived under the sky. I think it might take some time for me to adjust."

"Living outdoors isn't a bad thing. I'll be there with you."

"I know. I'm just saying a certain life was forced on us, and we lived in constant fear. Making this change is a good thing, but I think it may not be so easy to accomplish."

"We go a day at a time. They say changing habits usually takes thirty days. After a month, it will start to feel normal to be out and about."

"Is that another adage?"

"It is."

She turned her head to look back at the huge movement of her people all gathered in one place. "It's a sight I will never forget."

"You've done an incredible thing, conquering the Urghur. The corps couldn't do it."

She smiled slightly. "Yes, we did. It seems like a miracle."

"In a way, it was. We needed a lot of things to go right for us. For them, losing their air force was huge."

Turning her head, she took Brady's hand. "We had great inspiration from our E3T friends. You made us believe we could fight back and even win. We would never have come to that realization on our own. Life is so precious to us, making such sacrifices of lives stymied us into our old ways of hiding and cowering in fear. From this vantage point now, it seems so weak and stupid on our part."

"Honey, there isn't a creature alive that doesn't look back with regrets at their decisions. Nobody is right all of the time. It's probably hard for you to understand this, but for the first time, we of the corps feel free, and for the first time, we don't have another war to fight in an endless line of wars. The only way out of our army was always feet first."

"How can such a system endure? One would think it would collapse in on itself from inner rot."

"I can't disagree, and maybe that's their ultimate fate. I won't be sorry to miss being around them to see the spectacle. For the sake of countless billions living in that confederation, the sooner it happens, the better. However, the greatest probability is that the losers will just be replaced by other rich bastards who will take up where they leave off."

"That's a very distressing thought, Brady."

"It is."

"Do you believe there is a higher power? Our beliefs center on a supreme being."

"I wasn't a religious man in terms of going to religious services and so forth, but I did hold a level of faith in my heart. Contemplating on a being of infinite wisdom and power is a comforting thought when confronting the vast amount of evil in the universe. One would hope that there is an ultimate accountability, that in the end the evil ones get what's coming to them."

Beca eyed him, curious. "The dire fate of evil doers is what gives you comfort?"

"Well, I probably didn't say that very well. I do want justice for the oppressed."

Beca thought about the feelings expressed by her mate. "I guess I can't disagree with you. I just don't want it to affect us too much. The quality of the life we live is important to the Akara."

"That's a good trait. I'm fine with it. Perhaps being around you will make me a better man."

"You're a better man already. You don't need me for that."

As they walked, Brady got a sense of what life would be like living with the Akara. Untold citizens nodded to him in true reverence during the steady march home. For Brady, it was a little unsettling. Beca acknowledged the accolades briefly, but she tried her best to ignore the perplexing and unwanted notoriety.

"Are you ready for this?"

"I'm not sure. I've really never spent much time in the spotlight, and I was fine with that. Being somebody's hero or role model doesn't feel right. I don't deserve anybody's worship. They don't know me well enough to understand that fact. I suspect the more they're exposed to me, the less endearing I'll seem to them."

"I very much doubt that."

"You're my wife. You're required to be supportive."

She turned her head to look at him in mock outrage. "You're saying I can't make up my own mind?"

He chuckled. "No, of course not; my humor is still lacking."

"Good answer, sir. We've come a long way to gain equal status for females on this planet. We're not going to backslide now."

"You have, and I've supported you every step of the way. I'm on your side."

"You are?" She smirked. "I was just trying to joke with you also. Human comedy is still a puzzle for me."

"No problem. Human comedy is a puzzle for us too." He patted her back affectionately.

Rosca wandered over as they walked.

"Hello. Are you two agreeable to meeting with the council when we get home? We have much to discuss about what we should do next. Visule, our resident genius, has many ideas, bold ideas. Our elders can be set in their ways, so it has caused some ripples. I'm of the opinion we can't go back to the old ways, but the best alternative is difficult to discern. We need the help of our new friends."

"That's fine. I'm curious what kind of ideas Visule is suggesting. He is a brilliant guy."

"He heard about your teaching institutions and research facilities, so he would create our first universities, and he would also make a laboratory to study various things. He's talking about building factories and other facets from your world to make us modernized. Your weapons need ammo, so he proposes to make them."

"He's a man ahead of his time, no doubt about that. I know you're not a warlike people, and after the horror of this world war to wipe out the Urghur, it's an unsettling thought. However, you saw that you can't hide in a hole from evil. Preparing for what else might come down from the skies is the only logical path, in my opinion. I'm sorry for the changes to your society and to your sensibilities, but change comes to us, whether we want it or not. Also, change comes with a price tag."

"I agree with you, Brady. Although there will probably be resistance, that is mostly old men wishing for a gentler time for the future. That nostalgic idea may seem appealing, but it isn't realistic or sustainable. The old ways are gone forever."

Beca piped in. "That is a good thing. Females should never have been cast in subservient, lesser roles. It's time that we have our day."

Rosca smiled.

"You don't agree?" She eyed him harshly.

"Don't misunderstand me, Beca. I don't disagree with you. I'm just thinking about the ramifications for Akara society as it moves forward into this new social order."

Beca huffed. "Akara society will be just fine. It will be much better actually."

Rosca put up his hands like he was surrendering. "I'm not your enemy, Beca."

"I'm sorry if I come off badly, Rosca. It's been a sore point for me for quite some time. Please pardon me."

"Beca, we need your ideas too. I hope you can understand that change can take time. Those among us who have different points of view are entitled to express their feelings."

"That's fine, as long as they don't express their stupid feelings to me, or any other female. We're soldiers now and capable of bringing the pain."

Both men laughed heartily.

Brady replied, "Wow, Beca, cool your jets. We won the war, remember?"

"Well, gentlemen, we've put up with stodgy intolerance long enough. Thankfully, husband, we had your ladies to show us the way. The Akara women were pulled up out of the injustice of such ways and given a new lease on our lives. Believe me when I say we don't intend to squander the opportunity."

Brady patted Beca on her shoulder. "I'm with you, honey. Rosca, there's nothing in Visule's ideas I have any problem with. If we can manufacture ordnance to rearm our weapons, that would be a very good thing. Defending ourselves is a no-brainer."

"Visule is the eternal optimist, but I think implementing his plans will be very difficult. Making the leap into your technology from our primitive starting point seems incredibly daunting to me."

"You would be correct in that, but I'm not going to sell Visule short. What he can accomplish may surprise all of us."

Ironically, ahead of them, Visule was walking in the middle of a great number of younger Akara scholars, talking a great deal. He turned and noticed Rosca, Brady, and Beca, and slowed down to allow them to join his group.

"Hello, Beca."

"Hey, what about us?" said Brady in mock outrage. Beca laughed.

"I'm sorry, Brady, but your wife is so much more attractive, so logically, I would greet her."

"Thank you, kind sir," Beca replied.

"Rosca has mentioned some of your ideas. What would you do first?"

"I would create a science institute. I want to locate the best minds among our people and put them to work immediately. After the Urghur experience, I feel like we're vulnerable while in a primitive state. I wish to rectify that weakness in the shortest time possible."

"That sounds like a good idea. Visule, we of E3T are very impressed by you."

"Well . . . let's see if I warrant such high praise. You won the war, not me. Don't bother giving me some rationalization to soothe my ego. I don't require it. I'm a realist and that is reality. My part was never to be the warrior."

"In the end, your part will be the most important of all."

"We shall see. I hope you're right. Perhaps the Akara may someday warrant joining your confederation of planets."

"Let's not make it one of our initial goals. Believe me . . . we're far better off on our own. The leadership in the Federation is tainted and corrupt. If we go in that direction in the future, we've got to do it from a position of strength."

"As you wish, Brady. I accede to your knowledge and experience in that area."

Beca winced and made a soft sound.

Visule eyed her closely and then looked astonished when he realized what it was. "Beca, are you . . ."

"Yes, I'm pregnant."

"What?" said Brady. "We're going to have a baby?"

"Does that make you happy, my love?"

"Of course it makes me happy."

"Congratulations, Brady," said Rosca. "This is truly a blessed day for the Akara."

Brady suddenly frowned. "Wait a minute; you went into the fighting carrying our baby?"

"I did; it was my duty to my people to do my part."

"You could have—"

She scowled at him. "Drop it, please. It's over and done with. I'm fine, as is our child."

"You should have told me."

"If I did, you would have sent me to the rear. That wasn't acceptable."

"Not acceptable to whom?"

"I wasn't going to sit on the sidelines while others of my people died for our cause."

"Well, from now on we tell each other everything, and no more risk taking."

Beca smiled. "That's fine; however, I'm not fragile. It isn't necessary to treat me as such. I won't break."

"See that you don't."

Their route took them back to the cave, as all of the Akara returned to their hidden homes, although it was on a temporary basis. Plans to move to the surface began immediately as crews were sent out daily to scout ideal places for building new cities, towns, and villages. The E3T bases became focal points, with cities springing up around them, in addition to the other sites selected for development.

With their reverence for the environment, the Akara weren't a people to clear away the land of the native forest to any great extent; they only did what was necessary. They tried to incorporate the cities into the existing ground cover, and the animal wildlife was given plenty of territory to roam and replenish.

Agriculture was a new enterprise as the E3T taught the locals farming techniques, although those techniques needed to be fine-tuned to adapt to Akara particulars.

The Akara people went about the tasks of nation building with great diligence, and it was amazing to Brady how rapidly they made great strides. He was further amazed at the relative lack of interpersonal strife among the Akara. They got along much better than typical human societies.

As seems to happen so often after the conclusion of wars, with the huge loss of life, the survivors turned back to bonding and the propagation of the species.

Beca's two sisters, who were also war veterans, married, and in both their cases, they also chose E3T mates. Beca's two youngest sisters were still not of age yet.

Jocol was an exception to the usual Akara practices of monogamy. His culture didn't practice single-mate arrangements. Instead, they moved on to different partners without ramifications, as it was their norm. It led to greater genetic distribution and a stronger species.

He didn't formally marry any single female. He established friendships-with-benefits-type liaisons. It was radical, a shock wave that rippled throughout the straight-laced Akara society, but none objected to his face. Who could stand up against this giant who had single-handedly slain more Urghur soldiers than most others combined?

With the innate danger involved with his amorous interludes caused by natural frenzy of his people during intimacy, he arranged to be firmly tied down so he couldn't inflict any injuries to his partners in his intense fervor. His progeny would be unique hybrids among the Akara, huge by their standards, with a mix of Akara traits and with Jocol's traits.

Misty opted to pick Bontag as a husband, which mildly surprised Brady. Deluged with suitors, she was possibly the most sought-after female on the planet, since Beca was off the market, so to speak. Sara married another E3T soldier.

Sonya chose to be the first E3T woman to take a radical step by bonding in matrimony with an Akara, and she chose Visule. Already a planetary celebrity, landing an E3T human bride made Visule a living legend among his people. It invigorated him in his dreams for progress, and his science institute took shape soon thereafter.

Equally, part of building the new Akara cities included incorporating necessary E3T technologies. Incredibly, there were enough E3T troops with the knowledge necessary to implement the manufacturing processes. Using existing aircraft, weapons, and ammunition as samples, Visule and his collection of the finest minds among his people proved to be fast studies in learning how to duplicate the processes for making weapons of war. Having E3T mentors at hand greatly aided them in that process.

Later, the first time they were able to test the newly manufactured ammo with success, it was celebrated everywhere. Creating sufficient modern weapons to fully arm the Akara army gave them a feeling of security, as they had closed their gap of vulnerability.

Building an air force was a far more daunting challenge and required far more time. Just like with duplicating ground vehicles, Visule oversaw dismantling an aircraft down to the nuts and bolts and then implementing the manufacturing processes to make new parts. Fortunately, with the presence of E3T to help answer questions, new Akara forges and factories started to push out parts as well as ammo to allow for the creation of modern armaments for the protection of the planet in case of further off-world incursions. It wasn't an overnight happening; however, Brady was surprised at the rapid progress they made. Visule was no dummy, nor were his handpicked associates. The challenge of the tasks excited and stimulated them.

Sonya volunteered to be a test pilot in the first vessel to come off the assembly line. By that time, she had two children, which made her somewhat reluctant to take the risk. Visule was even worse in trying to handle the worry. For him, Sonya, as his wife, was a miracle he was hard pressed to release to the risk of the unknown testing of the new vessel. Realistically, they had no other viable choice. Sonya was the best pilot and the most capable of dealing with any possible in-flight issues.

Though the craft mostly functioned properly, it was still a frightening ride. However, once the minor adjustments were made, the Akara produced more craft to make the new air force. At that point, they only made planetary fighter craft. Although they discussed interstellar vessels, that was a project for later years.

Sonya and the other E3T pilots trained brave Akara to be pilots, and that included females.

After many years, the Akara "new world" was compared to the primitive life they had lived, but there was no comparison. The elders grumbled ceaselessly with each other about what they'd lost of their old lives, but the young had no patience for it. They embraced the progress wholeheartedly and in all aspects. The hybrid children were accepted fully, and in fact were treated as special. Jocol's progeny in particular were objects of great admiration. They retained enough of the traits of Jocol's people, so they required the strong hand of their father in their formative years to learn to rein in the more explosive aspects of their personalities. Teaching them to not be bullies by lording over their smaller contemporaries because they could proved to be a full-time job for him and for the mothers of each child.

"I'm sorry, my dear," Jocol said far too frequently to his many consorts to the challenges of raising his rambunctious offspring.

The Akara world had been altered irrevocably, and some thought that wasn't a good thing. Most, however, were on board with the changes. Social and societal mores needed to be flexible going forward, and that is what occurred. Although the Akara people coped with Jocol's unique issues, elsewhere the family unit remained generally a father and a mother in a monogamous bond.

A second major change to Akara society was the political structure of dispersed and independent, coexisting communities that eventually transformed into the E3T model of a single national government and a single overall ruler. It was a surprisingly difficult transition, as it came across as a foreign concept not suited to the minds of many of the Akara. Strangely, where the singular issue of Jocol mating with numerous females seemed to have been the thorny issue, it was not. The few scattered Akara who attempted to resume their old ways without a single federal government and leadership structure failed miserably. Considerable discussions of the matter tended to pit the older Akara against the younger Akara. However, it was clear very early the stalemate had to be broken.

The first thing the E3T members did was exempt themselves from ever being considered for political roles of leadership. The Akara would only be ruled by Akara.

Visule was the logical choice as first leader, though he fought it strongly. He wanted to do the work in his research centers. However, his people wouldn't accept his "no" answer, and soon he was installed as the first Akara head of state. Working in that job alone quickly proved to be too much for one man.

Later, out of necessity, Beca received a similar draft measure to become Visule's second-in-command. She too was given no option to reject the "honor." The ramifications for Brady was that now his wife lived far away, in the newly built capital city, the seat of the global, federal government. Meanwhile, Brady lived back in a far more rural location with the children, which at this point consisted of two sons and two daughters. Beca birthed her children in rapid succession, and their ongoing married life was interdicted by her call to duty, serving her people.

Grandma and Grandpa lived nearby, which spared Brady the sole duties of child rearing. Initially, it was a role he felt ill-equipped to handle, but with time and practice, he surprised himself at how much he came to enjoy dealing with his children.

After a lifetime of battle and stress, to be free to enjoy life was a happy development. It helped that his old E3T unit members opted to live nearby, so all of the children grew up together as friends. However, Brady's bed was still empty at night, and that challenge was an ongoing issue for him.

Misty found a marriage with Bontag to be very rewarding. He cherished her to the point she wondered why she'd waited so long to marry and told him so frequently. To say Bontag was gratified and pleased was an understatement.

Jocol lived in a massive building, one with many rooms to accommodate the menagerie that was his family. Life in that house was constant pandemonium, but the consorts helped each other to cope successfully in dealing with Jocol's wild offspring. They were unlike any children any Akara mother had handled in history. Regardless of the challenges, they were happy. It was an endless task, though, to teach those children not to bully their smaller Akara classmates, which was another first in this brave new world of diverse progeny. The nature of Jocol's race was innate aggression, so it was a never-ending test that endlessly required firm guidance from the father of the brood. Jocol didn't waver in doing his part in that area. He curbed his children's aggressive impulses, although he did hone their skills to be future warriors. His daughters were as unruly as his sons.

None of the E3T friends missed going back into battle as their life work. Freed at last from that odious and dangerous pursuit, they shifted gears to the joy of having and raising families. Having personal satisfaction and contentment finally, life seemed good. Life *was* good at that point.

Chapter Thirteen

With freedom from predation by the Urghur horde, guidance and help with modernization from the E3T survivors, the emergence of females in Akara society, all combined with the element of ample time, the world changed radically and rapidly. It wasn't rare to find females in positions of power and influence across the globe. That would have been unheard of prior to the arrival of E3T.

Schooling, in particular, experienced fundamental and profound changes. Although the Akara made a concerted effort to retain customs, practices, and beliefs from the old ways, it seemed inevitable modernization would dominate the new way, and it did. The young generation gave too little credence and respect to Akara lore, at least from the point of view of the elders. It was too easy to adopt the ways of off-world civilizations, whether societal mores and practices, career goals, or the buildup of a formidable military in case of further invasions.

Going to college was previously nonexistent and an unheard-of practice, but the idea came to dominate the thoughts and desires of the youth. College, as a new feature of the educational system, became the new ground to prepare for the future, and that included finding a mate. The ability of parents to have a significant role in choosing the person their children picked to marry ebbed greatly. Often, they were merely told after the fact by the children that they had made that lifetime choice.

With these vast societal changes, Visule was in full agreement, and as the first ruler of this world, it all but guaranteed the people were forced to accept it. With Sonya as a wife at his side, and with their revered hybrid off-spring, it was a strange dichotomy that the people still viewed them with messianic fervor, in spite of the ramifications of those major changes in their daily lives.

This new society of getting up each day to go to work, whether in factories, state facilities, schools, or mundane shops and other businesses, was a familiar environment for the E3T members, but for the Akara, coming from their hunter-gather roots, they felt nostalgic for what they'd lost as a simple society. The loss still emotionally plagued them.

New kinds of issues developed; they had taxation on their income to fund the new society and for grants to do research, competition in schools, and fame, with a focus on individuals. It was a direction the older Akara regretted. A society that had been oriented toward the group had now evolved to selfish thoughts and pursuits. There had been pervasive fear living under the Urghur, but now their children experienced a different kind of stress as they attempted to prosper at work and in their new world.

Visule spoke frequently with his wife and the other E3T members about the rumblings in the current society. Whether quiet discontent would remain quiet forever, he seriously doubted. Standing with Rosca, talking reflectively with Brady one day many years into the process, he spoke with concern.

"I can't believe we could become our own worst enemies."

Brady replied, "I tried to warn you about what we brought to the table. It was, and is, a double-edged sword. In our societies, we never solved these issues, so we can offer no guidance to you about coping. I'm hoping you're smarter than us and can figure it out on your own."

"I'm at a loss seemingly every day. Too many Akara citizens expect miracles from me. I can't make everybody happy."

"As trying as it is for you, honestly, I expected worse problems. I think you've done very well."

"Really? Perhaps because this is such a departure from how we were raised, I'm as concerned as any of the elders. The youth discount anything we say, like only they can know what's best. I've told Sonya how our females are trying so diligently to become like human women, that they've lost what was good about being an Akara. That includes more than just the young ones. The elders think I'm happy about that. I'm not."

"I know what you're saying. You're not alone in feeling that way. I suspect the elders of any race anywhere have similar feelings."

Rosca spoke, "No offense, but our youth see your ways as the only path with merit. Anything of the Akara is discounted or ignored."

"No offense taken, Rosca, transitioning is never easy. I would never pretend our way is superior, as I've explained in the past. However, I could stand up and preach to your young, yet I doubt it would make any difference to them."

"I agree with you. That's why I don't waste my time trying to do that very thing."

The men pondered for a moment, digesting the ideas. Brady spoke again. "I would like to add that our way is an amalgam of many societies. It isn't just a human thing. Maybe it sounds like I'm being defensive. I don't intend that. I guess I'm trying to add perspective."

"I understand, my friend. Perhaps I'm just airing my grievances. There is no wrong on your part."

"I appreciate your saying that."

"You're married to Beca, so you're one of the people. Our youth probably say I'm just a crotchety old man more suited for a rocking chair than teaching them anything."

The three chuckled.

"A rocking chair isn't a bad idea," Visule mentioned. "I like those few precious moments out of the eyes of the public. Their demands can be . . . difficult."

"Correct me if I'm wrong, but it seems moving to the surface has gone really well."

"It has, Brady. I thought feelings of vulnerability created by living out in the open would be far more difficult for Akara citizens, but I think it was mostly the older ones who struggled. The young adapt so quickly it astounds me."

Rosca spoke, "I believe you're right, Visule. We elders did have more of a challenge dealing with those feelings, but I think having every single one of those Urghur dead helped a great deal."

The men turned at the sound of children's voices. Brady's kids, as well as Visule's children, were running toward them. Hybrid children were not a negative factor in this society. They were great friends, and in fact, they were all seen with envy by their Akara classmates rather than as targets for bullying because they were different.

"Father, it's us," said Sadie, Visule's oldest daughter. Obviously, Sonya had named her.

"It's you, really?"

The children laughed.

"How was school today?"

"It was boring," said Beran, Brady's oldest son. Beca had named him. Sadie and Beran were born only months apart, so their lives were intertwined in nearly everything. They were very close in their friendship.

"Was it boring?" Brady asked Sadie.

"No, Beran was boring."

"Hey, I'm never boring," he retorted.

"Duh, get a clue, Beran."

The children raced off, with Beran chasing Sadie. Brady looked at Visule. "It's amazing how they've picked up our mannerisms and speech patterns. That could have been me talking back when I was young and in school."

Visule looked at Rosca. Rosca spoke, "It's exactly what we're talking about. The old ways of how Akara children acted and what they said seem to be gone. We're raising a race of your children."

"Is that bad?"

"Ultimately, no. It's just we wish both societies would survive rather than having your ways totally supplant ours. It's our nostalgia talking, not some great rebellion on our part."

"Okay, Rosca. By the way, I've told Beca she needs to teach Akara lore to our children. She agrees, but with her job and being away so much, it just doesn't happen. I've thought maybe I'd retain an Akara tutor locally. What do you think?"

"That could easily be arranged. Whether it would work for your children is another matter. Would they put up with it, as they say?"

"I'd be sure they do."

"Because Beca has been so kind as to accept the charge of the Akara people as my second, I've purposely tried not to impose on you, Brady. That way, at least one parent is always present in your children's lives. We could use your help in the defense industry, obviously. I never stop worrying about hostile new visitors from off-world. Our forces are far advanced from those primitive days, but we haven't been tested against skilled opponents. Do you think your military forces will come back some day with bad intentions?"

"Anything is possible. Although, I understand negotiations with the Federation are going well."

"That's true. We've applied for membership. It would solve a number of problems."

"I see no reason you wouldn't be accepted. The Federation has nothing to lose."

"I still worry about the Urghur race also; however, I think we could make it very difficult for them to establish any sort of foothold now. From the reports I get from the E3T trainers of our military, the Akara army is very good these days."

"That's a good thing."

"Our youth like to think of themselves as qualifying for membership in E3T."

Brady chuckled. "They give us far too much credit. Becoming jarheads isn't much of a positive."

"They would disagree."

"As you said, they're young, so they don't know any better."

"Those smart ones that prosper in your universities are the marvels, Visule."

"I'm very proud of them. They give us great hope for the future."

"Letting your females loose to pursue their dreams was the best decision you could make, in my opinion. There is great potential there."

"They do cut a wide swath, to use your words. The people would have no problem with Beca succeeding me."

"I don't think she wants that. Between you and me, I hope she doesn't. I realize I'm being selfish, wanting her just for myself."

"I'm just telling you the perception of her out in the world by the masses."

"I know. I understand how remarkable a wife I have. She's one of a kind. I was very lucky to get her."

"I feel the same way about Sonya. I'm still stunned she would accept me as her husband when she could have anybody."

"You made her happy. That's what is important. Being a wife and having kids suits her. Being the warrior wasn't a direction she wanted to continue for her entire life."

"I hope you realize how much Beca regrets the time away from you and her children."

"I know; she tells me. It's just a sacrifice we're forced to make at this point in time. Like it or not, building a modern nation is a difficult step and a long-term process. Here you had to start from scratch in every facet of society to have a modern world."

"Sadly, that's true."

"I hate that she's gone, living in the capital city, but we look forward to the day when somebody else steps up and takes the reins. I never thought I'd live the role of house-husband, but here I am. Honestly, though, it's not really a bad life, being with your children. It certainly beats going to war. Living with my wife would be really nice, though."

A sudden, loud roaring sound in the forest signaled the rapid approach of another powerful storm that shook the trees all about. With little warning and even less time to react, everybody raced for cover before the weather front could drench them. The daylight darkened considerably with the black clouds obscuring the twin suns.

It was one of the rare times when Beca could be home with her family. She smiled at Brady when he hustled in the door. All of their children were safely in the house and crowded around Brady in a group hug.

"You do well coping with our weather, sir."

"I've had plenty of practice, ma'am. It's nice to have you home."

"It's nice to be home. Being in the capital, people never leave me alone. There are always so many questions and issues. The demands on my time never end. It's fatiguing mentally."

"Well, you can relax here. Don't think about the job."

"Did I tell you, Visule's special appointees, the top graduates of his schools, they've finished building those long-range sensor devices. Once they turn them on, assuming they work, we can detect what is all around us in space. I'm sure they don't have as a long a range as your army, but we have some warning now if trouble is coming."

"Good. That's very good, honey."

"Our military command tells us we can defend ourselves now as we've become formidable with our armed services on the ground and in the air."

"That's also good to hear."

"Why are you smirking? In spite of our wholesale changes, do you think the Akara are still primitives? Literally, we're different in every possible way. Just looking at clothing for example; where before we all dressed to blend into the forest to avoid Urghur notice, now we wear modern fabrics and diverse colors. We dress like your people. We mimic your speech, habits, mannerisms, and ways of thinking. The old Akara culture seems to be passé. Did you fail to notice I'm wearing a stylish red dress for you?"

"No, of course not. I'm smiling because I said relax, and you're doing just the opposite."

Beca smiled sheepishly. "Of course, you're right. I'm in the work mode so much I don't even realize I'm doing it."

"No problem, darling. Why don't you go play with the kids while I cook up something special for us to eat?"

"Thank you, I'll do that."

They looked up as the children had eased up close by them.

"Dad, not victory stew again," his children complained in unison.

"Hey, that's good eating, folks."

"Not every night it isn't."

Beca laughed and hugged her husband.

"Your children need to get a clue, madam. Victory stew is a classic, fine cuisine by any definition."

"So, they're *my* kids now?"

"Yeah, unless they agree with me they are."

"Right. You realize I'm no longer a silly adolescent agog to be in your presence."

"I do."

"That means your poor attempts at humor fly like a lead balloon, to use your words. The concept of addled comes to mind."

"I know that too."

"Yeah, Dad," said his oldest son.

"Butt out, dude. This is big person talk."

"Big person? Do you mean Mom?" All the children laughed.

"You are cruisin' for a bruisin', little man." Brady shook his fist in mock outrage.

Brady made a move toward his son, who laughed and darted out of the way.

"You're the one who created them in your image," said Beca wistfully.

"That's true."

"They're just like you."

"Probably. However, I'd like to point out, although I was a handful as a child back home, I turned out okay."

"You did? I hadn't noticed."

"Very funny."

She laughed heartily along with the children.

"Mom got you, Dad," his oldest daughter added.

"She did; no doubt about it. Well, I'll pass on making the stew and think about making something else. You guys move along now and let me go to work."

"Thank you, husband. That is very thoughtful of you to do this for us."

"My pleasure."

His oldest daughter spoke, "Can I help you, Dad?"

"Okay, honey. Are you sure you don't want to go play with your mom and siblings?"

"Naw, my siblings are a pain. I won't abandon you, Daddy."

Sadie's statement struck him for some reason. Her love for a father evoked his warm inner feelings; it was another example of his transition from consummate warrior to compassionate family man. The genuine emotions of the love of a family warmed his heart. These precious beings, a loving wife and his children, gave him meaning in his life that didn't exist previously. Brady couldn't resist grabbing his little daughter in a firm hug.

"Daddy, I can't breathe."

"Sorry."

"That's okay, you can mash me as much as you want. I love you, Daddy."

He mashed her again, although this time he adjusted the strength of his firm embrace.

"I love you too, darling."

Beca was smiling warmly. "This is such a great life we have together."

"I agree, honey. Okay, let's get this party started."

He went to the kitchen with his daughter, while Beca rounded up the other children in the living room.

"What are we making?" asked Sadie.

"I'm open to your suggestions, since you didn't like any of my ideas."

"Can we make a human meal?"

"What did you have in mind?"

"Grilled cheese and soup, and can we have pie for dessert?"

"Okay, that's easy enough to make. As far as the dessert, you're lucky it's already baked, but you knew that, you little imp."

She snickered. "We all know that, Dad. It smelled so good when it was cooking, we wanted to eat it right then, straight out of the oven."

"I hear that. I know what you mean."

Later, when they sat down as a family at the dinner table, Beca mentioned, "What a change from my childhood. These modern meals are so different from what we had when I was a child."

"I hope that's a good thing."

"It is, Brady. In the capital city, we all eat these kinds of meals and have come to like them very much. It's not a bad thing. Now, having the traditional Akara meal is very rare."

"I'm happy to hear that."

"In the old days, under the Urghur, obviously we had severe limitations on a great deal of things. Our hunters took their lives in their hands every time they went outside of the cave to look for food. I'm glad my children don't live in such a world."

The children ate, oblivious to the conversation of their parents. Such weighty matters didn't draw the attention of their young minds yet. In fact, the life of this family resembled that of Brady's childhood far more so than Beca's childhood.

"For us, farming is like a miracle. Growing crops of our choice on the surface for harvest, it's revolutionary."

"You would have farmed if you had had access to the surface back then. It would have been an inevitable development. A civilization has got to be able to feed the populace."

"Our ancient ancestors probably farmed prior to the Urghur invasion."

Taking a step onto tenuous ground about his secret, inner feelings, Brady tried to sound casual. "By the way, how is Bralic doing in running the military? Does he mind being stuck at the capital?"

Brady had noticed over time that Beca always smiled when the topic of Bralic came up. When she spoke about him, it was warm and effusive. On this day, she missed noticing his simmering angst when she replied. For Brady, she sounded affectionate about Bralic.

"He's doing very well. I think he learned a great deal in the war and from the E3T people in particular. And we learned more than just the military side, all the new ways of living modern lives. In my opinion, I think he does not mind living in the city. He's a dear friend who I depend on a great deal. We get along very well and are both contented with our current circumstances."

"I'm surprised he hasn't gotten married." Brady took a further step onto dangerous ground, like he was feeding her rope. Still, she had yet to pick up on his inner feelings of distress.

"I . . . eh, we talk about it. He didn't feel the right woman was . . . well . . ." She stammered as it dawned on her finally that he was upset. Brady's pinched tone and grim facial expression caught her notice.

"Beca, I know he wanted you as his wife. You can say it out loud." The defeatist way he spoke it befuddled her.

She took a moment to ponder before she replied, speaking honestly. "Yes . . . that's no secret. It was nothing I had against him as a potential mate. He's as impressive as any Akara male in the world, perhaps ever. I liked him very much, and I still do now. However, I was agog over you early on, and those feelings never changed. Bralic is content at this point with having our nice friendship. We eat our meals together. When our daily work is done, I enjoy his company in the evenings, and he likes mine. It helps having a close friend to cope with the loneliness in the midst a crowd, if you understand what I mean by that. He's trustworthy with my truths, so I can share anything with him. He has a nice way about him, very intriguing."

"I do understand that."

She eyed his contemplative, questioning look. "Is there a problem, Brady?"

"He spends far more time with you than I do."

"I know that, but we knew the challenges when I accepted this position. Perhaps there's something in human views or emotions about this that I'm missing? I'm not sure what I'm sensing in you."

At that point, Brady held back on what could be termed whining, as he glanced at his children in their midst. They didn't need to hear it. Whether the Akara had the same equivalent feelings of jealousy as humans, he couldn't say, and the family dinner table was no place to discuss it.

"Bralic is a good guy, no worries. It's fine, Beca."

His words said one thing, but his tone and the look on his face seemed to say the opposite. She frowned in dismay.

"I think . . ."

"Little ears," he whispered.

"Then perhaps we should talk later."

"Perhaps we should."

The remainder of the meal was consumed in relative silence, except for the children. Beca glanced at her husband frequently. She felt ill at ease at the unexpected, awkward moment that she hadn't seen coming.

Once the children were asleep in their rooms, Brady and his wife continued their private conversation before bed. With the bedroom door closed, they were freed to discuss the matter.

"Brady, I think I don't understand this, whatever this is."

"I've never been married before, so I've never dealt with the emotions that go along with it, and I've never tried to cope with our particular dynamics where you live away. As strong as you see me as the tough soldier, this seems to be my Achilles heel."

"What does that mean? I don't know that reference."

"It's from mythology on my home world. It refers to my weakness or vulnerability."

"Okay, but you need to explain this to me. Do you see me in error in some way? Have I done something wrong?"

"I'm not saying that. I'm also not saying that my feelings reflect how any human male would react. I didn't even know myself about this particular facet of my psyche."

"What is it that is the problem?"

"On my world, in the dynamics of our social interactions, it's not unheard of that women working closely with men can develop relationships over time."

"Relationships? I do have relationships with many people. Are you saying that is bad?"

"What I'm talking about in the context of human society is that some women can develop certain feelings for those men, men they're not married to. With time enough in being together, things can happen."

"Things?"

"Intimate things."

Beca looked at him, astounded. "I'm not sure what to say to that. I'm married to you, Brady."

"I'm talking about feelings. Do you see? We're apart most of our time, and I'm not there in the capital city to see your actions."

Beca's expression changed abruptly, hardening into anger. "What are you saying, that I look to be with Bralic in that way? That I already have perhaps?"

Brady felt miserable. It was the last thing he wanted to do, making her feel he was accusing. He couldn't manage a reply.

"I'm not a human woman in the context you're describing. I don't look to dishonor our marriage. I would think you'd know that."

"Beca, I'm sorry. I wasn't implying you're doing anything bad."

"Really? It certainly sounds that way to me."

"I was trying to explain my feelings. Feelings are not always rational."

"I see. You've given me a great deal to think about, husband."

Her grim stare wasn't reassuring. She continued, seething. "Perhaps we shouldn't share the same bed tonight."

Brady nodded his head sadly. "It's my bad, Beca. I'll sleep on the couch."

Provoked, she turned away, in no mood to be forgiving.

As he walked to the door, she added, "I guess I was wrong. Even after all of these years together, it seems you don't understand the Akara."

"You're probably right."

He closed the door to the bedroom as he left.

Sleep didn't come quickly that night for Brady. Shooting himself in the foot, so to speak, had been a foolish move. Brady's mind struggled. *Without proof of wrongdoing, why did I even bring it up?* He had no answer to that question, he tossed and turned, and no answer came to him, yet his mind wouldn't release him into sleep.

Alone in her bed was her norm in the capital, but not at home. Beca pondered the unexpected incident also, but through a completely difference perspective. Living two lives, one of mother and wife, and the other of celebrity and high government official, which isolated her from that family, she did make some choices to cope over time. Keeping those two lives distinctly separated had always seemed to work, at least until now. Actually, her life had worked well for her. It was Brady having issues that had never crossed her mind. In fact, the reality was the Akara citizens had learned everything the E3T members taught them, and that included the dark side of their off-world societies. It wasn't that marital strife was unheard of among the Akara, as some pairings weren't ideal, and mates did look in other directions. However, with the dynamics of life in fear of the Urghur where the Akara, by necessity, lived in close proximity, it wasn't exactly the same problem as that faced by humanity. In socially open environments, humans were freer to potentially explore poor options with questionable choices.

Her life in the capital was unprecedented for Akara society, and these days she wasn't alone in that type of life. Living apart from her mate for lengthy time spans hadn't occurred before in Akara history. It was new ground in so many ways. *Having a close friendship with Bralic, is it wrong?* She pondered about him and other things too, and it irked her. It delayed her also in finding rest for the night. *Is my strong emotional bond cheating? Is Brady right? Are there possible future poor choices lurking for me? Could I actually fall prey to . . . ?* The troubling ideas haunted her.

Suddenly, those impossible mistakes didn't seem so impossible if she was honest about it. It was an unnerving idea. Though her mind could grasp the fallacy, it was too easy to blame humans for problems, including increased emotional vacillations. That included a childish desire to punish her husband, even though he'd done nothing wrong. Taking action against him would only fester and complicate the matter. Deciding against it, she realized there were other ways, better ways, to alleviate her ire.

Rolling over finally after some time, and further considerations, Beca still fell asleep far sooner than her husband.

Brady awoke in the morning poorly rested, awakened by his littlest child pouncing on him.

"Daddy," said his youngest daughter as she landed on his sleeping body. "Are you awake?"

"I am now."

"Why are you on the sofa?"

"Mom needed some space last night."

Sitting up and looking, he saw the bedroom door was still closed. Rubbing his sleepy eyes, he hugged his little daughter and muttered, "Let's let Mom sleep until she's ready to get up."

"Okay, but can we eat now? I'm hungry."

"Sure. Do you want to go out to hunt and trap an animal for breakfast?"

All of his children laughed.

Chapter Fourteen

When Beca finally emerged, breakfast for everyone else was done, and the children were outside.

She went to pour a cup of coffee.

"I've got some food still warm in the oven for you."

"Thank you," she whispered.

After she was seated at the table, eating her breakfast, he sat down with his cup of coffee.

"Beca, I'm sorry. I came across as an ass last night. Can you forget it and put it out of your mind?"

She continued eating and looking at her plate of food. After more bites, she finally answered. "Okay, Brady. If that's what you want from me, I absolve you." Her facial expression remained icy.

"I wasn't looking to open a can of worms, honey. When you asked for an explanation of my feelings, I should have known to keep my mouth shut. Talking intelligently about this kind of stuff is not my strong suit. I apologize."

She still stared at her plate; her cool reactions gave Brady a queasy feeling. What it could mean he wasn't sure, and he worried. Beca never acted moody.

Once her meal was done, she finally looked at him. "I didn't expect this, but I must admit, in this new world, and virtually every day, there is a great deal I don't expect for me to deal with. I think I need to ponder this for a time. Is that acceptable to you?"

"Whatever you need, darling. I'm sorry if I've added to your worries. As I said, it wasn't my intention. I think you drew the short straw marrying me."

There was the slightest hint of a smile, but what she was thinking, he had no clue. It was clear to him he'd struck a nerve. *Was it possible she . . . no, it couldn't be.* His mind punished him with the discordant thought. However, his own reassurances weren't particularly reassuring. Correctly interpreting females wasn't his strength.

"Can we do something to take our minds off this?"

"What did you have in mind?"

"How 'bout some family thing, like being with the kids to play some games?"

"Okay, Brady."

Her smile at that point looked to be forced and insincere. Rather, the fact she was still irked was clear for Brady to grasp. She stood up from the table. "Excuse me while I get ready for the day."

Going back into the bedroom, Beca closed the door. Usually, she would have invited him to join her in bathing for the day. Husband and wife together time was precious in their circumstances, with her gone so often. Silently spurning him, it was a new dynamic in the marriage, a troubling one from his perspective.

Outside, he could hear the shouts of his children at play. He wandered over to the window. His oldest child, Sadie, tended to try to lord over the others. She shared the same name as Visule's daughter. His oldest son, Beran, would have no part of that, and often the two clashed. His next youngest child, a son named Dran, tended to follow the older brother he idolized. Again, Beca had named the sons and Brady the daughters. The baby in the family was little Lily. She tended to shout a lot and chase around her bigger siblings. Those were the first names of Brady's two grandmothers.

Instead of waiting for Beca to emerge, Brady went outside. It was a sunny day, which wasn't the usual state of weather on this world. Atmospheric turbulence was the norm.

Lily raced over immediately to wrap him up with a hug. More accurately, she could only wrap up his legs with her small size.

"Daddy," she muttered.

"Hey, baby girl, are you having fun?"

"Yes, but they always try to run away and leave me behind."

"Well, you can play with me, okay?"

The other kids came over. Beran asked, "Where's Mom?"

"She's still getting cleaned up. She'll be out soon."

"Is she going away again?"

"Of course, that's her job."

"I want to have a job away too," said Sadie.

"You don't like living with me?"

"That's not what I mean. You can come and live with me, Daddy. I was just saying I want to be famous too, like Mom."

"You should ask your mom about that, if it's such a great life being apart. I don't know, maybe it is."

At that moment, Beca walked up.

"What was the question?"

"Sadie wants to live away and be famous. I told her you've already got that and you could give her some valuable insight."

Beca's stare at Brady was icy for a moment before she turned to her eldest and smiled. "Well, honey, it's got good points and bad points. I'm very busy, so time passes rapidly. I have important things to deal with, but on the other hand, I don't see my family every day. I have to cope with that, and it's very difficult."

"Oh," said Sadie. "I didn't think of that. Why don't we all live with you in the capital city?"

"Your father and I talked about it beforehand. We decided the best life for you is in this relaxed setting out of the spotlight and the hustle and bustle there. I'm taking the hit of living there rather than all of us taking that hit. Life in the capital isn't like life the Akara have ever had. Do you understand?"

"I guess." Sadie looked puzzled.

Brady added, "When we had that discussion, her living apart was supposed to be a temporary thing. It's blossomed in ways we didn't anticipate, so now we're not sure when it will end, or if it will end."

"Of course it will end," Beca replied, eyeing him dourly.

Brady added, "In my society, leaders are elected periodically. That isn't really the case here. Visule and your mom are on the hook for the duration, however long that might be."

The children looked at Beca, who bristled slightly.

"That's true to an extent. What your father didn't explain is that we're working on rectifying that issue. I don't want to live away forever, and Visule prefers getting back to his research at his institutes. There will be new leadership at some point in time. Though it's true we can't say when, it will happen as soon as we can arrange it. I miss you guys."

Eyeing Brady like she dared him to disagree, he simply stared back at her.

"What are we going to do now?" asked Dran. The adult's issues were going completely over his head.

His parents smiled at him. Brady spoke, "Let's play war. Get the ball, Dran."

"Girls against the guys," Sadie clarified. "Come on, Mom."

"Sure," she replied, smirking at Brady. "You're going down, dudes."

"We'll just see about that, madam."

It was a perfect tonic to get their minds off their unfortunate and troubling thoughts. Both adults allowed the children to make the bulk of the tosses.

After the game ended and the family trooped into the house for a midday meal, Beca seemed relaxed at last.

"This is how I want my life, Brady. Don't you see that?"

"As I said before, I'm sorry I irked you. It's my flaw, but I thought you needed to understand. I wasn't going to try to hide it and then have these feelings build up and explode at some point. I'm sorry, but I love my wife."

"I love you too. Is that even a question in your mind?"

"That's not it. Because I'm human and grew up in a human society, I was exposed to the faulty side of people. There were . . . problems within my family . . . some poor choices, and it led to real trouble. Maybe it warped me about having trust issues about certain areas."

"I'm sorry that happened to you."

"Being away so long, lonely, it can bring out some queasy feelings. I'm somebody that would rather know the truth than be in the dark."

She got a troubled look. "I'm not sure what to say about that. I appreciate your being honest, but from my point of view, it seems you don't trust me, and if that's true, well, it would be very troubling for me. I'm not trying to say I'm perfect, but what you're worried about, I'm not sure what I've done to warrant such concerns."

"Please understand, I'm not accusing you of anything. I'm just saying those are my feelings. In essence, what could I ever do about it anyway? When you're away, only you have control of your actions. Therefore, if you make decisions in private, in the dark, only you know it. If you choose to share what you do, and with whom, it is your decision."

"I don't think I'm getting across my feelings. From what you've explained, I would guess the norms in your human society are that you were raised very differently than Akara society. Maybe it's trouble on the horizon for us, as a society in transition, as we evolve closer to human ways of doing things. My opinion at this point is we still retain our strict and stodgy old ways in those areas of your concern. I can't speak for all of my people, but that's my opinion."

"I can respect that. Do I get admission back into our bedroom tonight? Lily landing on me like a ton of bricks in the morning when I was sleeping on the couch was a bummer."

Beca chuckled. "Fine, you can come back to bed."

"Thank you."

"I really would like to resolve this issue, though."

"I also."

"What would it take for you to trust me?"

"I do trust you, but you're not the only dynamic here."

"So . . . you don't trust Bralic? I don't understand."

"It's not that I don't trust him . . ."

"That wasn't very convincing, sir. Is it you expect me to have no male friendships? How could I do that, or any woman for that matter?"

"I told you, feelings aren't always rational, especially with the added element of such long stretches of time apart."

"Do you want to reconsider where you live and move the family to the capital city?"

"We both agreed on a simpler life for the children here, out of the spotlight. That hasn't changed."

"Well, Brady, the reality is the both of us are forced to make difficult choices. I love you and my children and look forward to getting back here, but if I get this kind of reception when I come home, it isn't going to work for me. Do you understand?"

He got a troubled look.

"Only you can deal with your jealousy demons. I don't know what to tell you. If I'd accused you of taking up with a female around here . . ."

"Of course I wouldn't."

"Well then, can you understand my anger?"

"Yes. I already said I'm sorry."

"I trust you and know you wouldn't do such things to me. Is it so hard to comprehend the same for me?"

"No, it isn't hard to comprehend. I'll do my best to keep my mouth shut from now on."

She eyed him pensively. "I don't think we've solved this. I think you want to do the worst possible choice, which is burying your feelings, which would lead to that explosion you mentioned. This concerns me a great deal."

"I'm sorry I brought it up. Why don't we table it for now?"

"I'm not happy about this."

"Beca, I do know that. You've got to leave soon, so let's savor this little time we have left."

"Okay. For your information, when I go back, I turn around immediately to accompany Visule to the test site for the first launch of an Akara interstellar vessel. They've gone as far as they can with testing on the planet without actually flying it."

"Oh, well stay back out of danger in case it blows up."

"Visule isn't stupid. He will have made proper arrangements for our safety. We wouldn't attempt a flight if the vessel wasn't ready."

"I know. I'm just saying sometimes things don't go as we planned. I've seen plenty of that in my life."

"Thank you for the concern, but I'll be fine."

"Is the whole staff going?" He said it without looking at her.

She eyed him grimly. "Yes, Bralic will be going too. He is the commander of our military forces after all."

"I was just curious."

"Right," she replied tersely.

"Okay, we drop the matter. I'll leave it in your hands, honey."

Beca remained irked. She muttered something softly, but Brady wisely didn't inquire as to what she said. It wasn't hard to figure out.

* * * *

Beca was genuinely sad to leave them behind when she boarded the transport craft for the flight to the capital city.

Beca hugged each of her children warmly, and she even hugged her husband tightly, though she still wanted to slug him. Looking out the transport window at them on the ground, a husband and four children looked up sadly, watching the transport craft take off and then turn toward the distant destination. She thought about them for a time, but pondering her job quickly took over her thoughts.

"Okay, gang, let's head home," Brady muttered.

Brady led the way as they trooped away from the landing field. Beca's idea of the family moving to the capital city crossed his mind for a moment, but he quickly dismissed it. As challenging as it was for him personally, this life away from the spotlight was better for the children, so he'd continue to take the hit for their sakes. Nothing was resolved, and nothing had changed in his married life at that point. His jealousy was still alive and well, even though he could conceive of the possibility that it was unwarranted.

* * * *

When Beca landed at the airfield in the capital city, she carried a different perspective. Bralic was waiting in the terminal, smiling and obviously anxious to see her. Examining her own feelings, the fact that she looked forward to seeing him too resonated. This time, however, Beca tempered any enthusiastic response, even when he swept her into his arms too firmly and for too long. He was not her husband, a fact she pondered at last in the midst of his fervor.

"Oh Beca, I missed you so much."

"It's good to see you also, Bralic."

When he didn't receive a usual firm hug equal to his effusive embrace, he looked at her face. "Is something wrong?"

"Eh . . . maybe we'll talk later. This isn't a good place to get into it."

"Okay. However, you know our schedule. We have a rapid turnaround before heading to the test site. Visule is already waiting for us, as well as the rest of the staff."

"I know. We'll find a minute somewhere in a less public setting."

Bralic looked confused and then looked around at the numerous people eyeing them. Celebrity was an uncomfortable burden new to the Akara.

"Certainly, Beca, whatever you say."

She noted the confusion on his face; adding her burden to him wasn't her desire. However, solving the problem for Brady wasn't a matter she could avoid or ignore. There were adjustments needed in her life, though omitting every facet of her separate existence would not work. Bralic would be a casualty where other personal choices would not be. Compromise was the best she could do.

Returning to their residences, he carried her luggage into the privacy of her rooms, as he always did. Being alone with her evoked him, and he suspected it moved her too. It had been a long-term, dangerous dance at the boundaries of propriety.

Beca turned to him. They stared for a moment as she tried to compose herself to express her thoughts as gently as she could with this difficult subject.

"I need to share with you . . . about my visit home. Eh . . . Brady surprised me by sharing his thoughts and feelings about certain matters. As you know in my marriage, we made a decision about living apart long ago because of the children. Presently, they have a simpler life, living away from the city and away from public scrutiny. For Brady, that was a big sacrifice. I assumed he handled it better than he actually has. I'd say with time passing certain things started to bother him, and it simply got worse."

"What things?"

"You can't guess?"

"Eh . . . maybe I could guess, but you should tell me."

"He worries about our relationship. We've become close, very close. When we talk together at home as spouses, it comes out in what I say about you. You're usually my main topic of conversation. I don't realize I'm doing it, but he's on the receiving end, and it doesn't strike him well."

"Beca, I won't pretend I have no feelings for you."

"For me, coping with being apart was always difficult, and with time, perhaps I should have known there could be ramifications. He explained he feels . . . jealous, that perhaps there are poor decisions going on."

Bralic looked worried. "I . . . eh . . ."

"We've been on a gradual path, so our steps have been slow and incremental; however, Brady made me stop to think about where we are. I spend most of my time with you, Bralic, not with my husband. We are very familiar now, as you know. I will also admit that I have feelings for you." She paused, eyeing Bralic. "Eh . . . also, he mentioned you've never gotten married."

"I . . . Beca, you were the woman I desired, but he was always between us. This life here was the next best thing for me. Imagining you as my wife, yes, I think about it a great deal. I believe you've had similar imaginings. I sense it in you."

"I didn't realize how we were seen by others. Look at our meeting just now at the airfield. How many people saw that warm, sustained hug? Did we look to be friends or something more to those other people? Technically, we haven't crossed any dangerous lines, but in his mind, Brady worries we will, if we haven't already. Do you understand, more than just Brady may think we already have? For me, that is a serious problem. Possibly it is of my own doing, as I look at it with different eyes."

"What is it you want for us to do?"

"Perhaps it would be wise if we act with better forethought and use better decorum, especially in public. I'm the wife of another man, so I need to reflect that fact."

She paused and turned directly to Bralic before continuing. "The truth is, at times we've come too close to those poor choices Brady worries about. Our emotions have been aroused in ways we should not have allowed."

Bralic frowned in dismay. "I'll honor your wishes, though I must tell you it will be very difficult for me. You're a vital part of my life. You know that."

"I know, and I worry I've abetted this situation. Where you could have found contentment, marriage, and a family with another woman, I allowed you to focus romantically on me. I was selfish in dealing with my own loneliness."

"Beca, you're one of a kind. There just aren't any other females that measure up."

"That's not true. As I said, I think we need to act with greater dignity, and you should begin to look around at other options."

His face was conflicted as he stared at her in helplessness. She had no words for the moment, so she turned her back. "I'll see you later at the transport."

"Okay," he whispered.

Waiting until she heard the door close, with her own emotions astir, she relaxed her tense stance, letting out the air she had been holding in her lungs. It was a loss for her too, this deep personal connection she was trying to sever.

"Are you happy, Brady?" she muttered childishly. "I've hurt my dear friend."

Lying down on her bed to ponder the issue, she wondered if she was the first Akara female to face this kind of test. "What a world you've brought to us, husband."

Pondering all the aspects of her life in the capital, her petulance emerged, hardening her decision to retain her other choices. However, her ruminations were short, and soon she sat up and got ready to leave on the next leg of her journey. After living through the life-threatening existence of combating the Urghur and potential annihilation, to be faced with this kind of issue now struck her badly, like it was unfair and she didn't deserve it. Was she not entitled to enjoyment in her life also?

"Brady," she muttered, "why are you doing this to me?"

Steeling her troubled emotions, she went out her bedroom door. However, her troubling thoughts went with her. What had been impossible previously under the control of close family proximity, now was possible. The Akara now had the benefit and the curse of free will and all of the temptations that went with it. Within her mind, Beca pondered the truth of her situation. *In its current form, is my relationship with Bralic appropriate?*

Although there were no blatant, physical violations of her marriage vows, her emotional connection was undeniable, and he filled the void of a missing husband. *Have I gone too far? Is it possible there could be future steps?* Saying to herself she wouldn't stray wasn't reassuring. Bralic occupied a warm spot in her heart, and he was certainly a very appealing male.

Arriving at the transport for her flight, Visule was already there talking to key assistants. Turning his head, he smiled as she walked up.

"Hello, Beca. It's nice to see you. Are you ready for this?"

"I'll tell you after the launch attempt."

Visule chuckled. "I know what you mean. We think the ship is ready, but this is the acid test."

Climbing onto the transport ship, Bralic was already seated. It was usual Beca sat beside him every time. She saw him looking at her sadly, and so did Visule.

Turning her head to Visule, she asked, "May I sit with you on the flight?"

"Certainly." He glanced at Bralic, who turned his head away. "Is there something wrong?"

"No, I just decided to enjoy your company this time."

"I don't know how enjoyable I am. However, you're welcome to put up with my nattering. You know I can't keep my mouth shut."

Beca smiled. "Thank you, Visule."

Once they were seated and the ship launched, he asked. "Is there something you want to talk about?"

She pondered spilling the beans. Getting it off her mind had great appeal, and Visule was someone she could trust.

"On my visit home, I had an unanticipated situation with Brady. As you know, we live apart for the children to live in a less public setting than the capital city. However, he shared his feelings of worry."

"Worry?"

"We live apart most of the time, and with as long as we've done that, he feels that perhaps I've become too close with Bralic."

"Too close? Oh . . . you mean in an inappropriate way."

"Yes, that was his worry. I haven't done that, and I wouldn't, but being married to a human, there are challenges. Their ways have bled into Akara culture, so I can't simply dismiss it. Honestly, I do feel strongly for Bralic. He's been there for me as a companion with Brady living back home. He made the statement that Bralic has never married, and he wooed me before I married Brady. I hadn't looked at the circumstances that way, through Brady's eyes. Now I wonder."

"Bralic is a good man."

"He is, however, with whatever he wishes . . . am I vulnerable to a future fall?"

Visule looked worried. "Only you can answer that, my dear."

"It makes me think I need to make changes. I don't want to hurt Bralic, but if we went on this way and had a . . . mishap, I couldn't live with myself. I'm the mother of four beautiful children, and the second to you as head of our people. Such a betrayal would be unprecedented and unworthy of the wife of my wonderful husband, and a great war hero. Do you see?"

"I understand. Beca, you're probably the most alluring Akara female in our history. I can understand Bralic's fascination, but if you think there could be bad possibilities, you're right to look at implementing changes in your relationship."

"I wish he could find a wife of his own. I don't want to end our friendship, but I don't think it's wise for us to be alone together any longer. I acknowledge I can be tempted also. I *have* been tempted. I should have realized it before now."

"Are you reconsidering your role in this government?"

"Honestly, I want to do my duty for the people, but my selfish side says, 'enough, it's somebody else's turn to bear the burden.' Do you understand?"

"Completely, I've also had feelings about retiring from public scrutiny to enjoy my wife and children. My marriage with Sonya is incredible. Obviously, in my case, they live here with me, so it's not the same situation you face. We've talked about moving away also to find a simpler pace in a less congested area."

"Do you think the people would allow us to leave?"

"They'd have no choice. My worry is leaving behind too much unfinished business. Building a proper space fleet for our protection is critical, in my opinion. There are too many threats out there to relax now."

"I understand, and honestly I agree with you. Whether I'm critical in that effort, like you are, I doubt it."

"Beca, if you choose to go home, I'm not going to stand in your way. You've given selflessly of your time, your ideas, your unique personality and presence, so there is no defensible reason to hold you back other than my own selfishness."

"Visule, you're not selfish. I've depended on you as much as the other way around. You're the greatest Akara person in our history."

Visule sputtered, "Please . . . I'm just another bumbling male."

"Hardly. You're a living legend and an icon."

"Right, in my own mind maybe." He chuckled. "Isn't it funny how much we talk like them now?"

"I know."

"I wouldn't go back."

"Nor I, but you know what I'm saying. As far as decisions, I'll stay at my post in the short term, but I think I'll start to look for possible replacements. I'm not willing to take the chance I could be my own worst enemy with doing something foolish."

"I accept your stance. You do whatever you feel you must, Beca."

Arriving at the test site, the dignitaries went to the bunker to watch the proceedings in safety.

Four heavy transports helped in drawing the huge vessel skyward out of the assembly bay, as the space drive couldn't be used on the planet. The interstellar vessel could only employ maneuvering jets in the planet's atmosphere and gravity field. Once they got into space orbiting the planet, the balance of the sizeable crew boarded the ship to begin the test run. This wasn't a ship similar to the Federation's massive, round space transports. It was built from the data supplied by Visule and his team of researchers. That meant a much different design, sleek and elongated.

The moment had arrived, the acid test, and the moment of truth. It was the culmination of a great deal of hard work. Could Akara genius prove equal to the challenge of emergence into intellectual equality with their off-world neighbors?

Igniting the engines, it functioned perfectly, and in an instant the ship was gone on the maiden voyage. Bralic, Visule, and Beca looked at each other and smiled at the success.

Beca spoke, "I'll admit, I was worried we would have a great tragedy and terrible loss of life."

Visule replied, "We all felt that way."

On impulse, facing them together, Beca continued, "Gentlemen, I've decided my future path should be at home with my husband and children. I've robbed them too much already, living away as I do. That's over."

"We understand," said Bralic sadly.

"I'll help you in the search for a successor, Beca," said Visule.

She turned to Bralic. "You've been such a dear friend. I couldn't have born up under this life without you. However, now I need to move on. I hope you can feel free to pursue your own happiness in the arms of another, without having to carry the burden of my—"

"Beca, say no more. I know why you feel you must do this. I'll be fine. Think no more about it."

"Thank you, Bralic. You'll always be dear to me."

* * * *

Months later, with a new woman installed in her place at long last, Brady had his wife back again. For him, it was like a miracle, as all of the long years of separation were over, and Beca gave him her love and full attention. That, he liked very much.

Bralic did find a woman, married, and moved on with his life also. Visule found it harder to get his own replacement, but a year later, he too moved on to his passion, working and researching at his institute.

The Akara planet had been newly admitted as a full-fledged member of the Federation. Supposedly, they were "blossoming," although the legacy of social issues that came with the ascension out of a primitive state into a modern society was a stark contrast. In a sense, it was a double-edged sword. Suddenly, having considerable traffic from all over the universe coming to visit, it was a new world in every sense of the word. Those visitors brought a variety of issues, along with the commerce of their purchases of goods and services. The Akara built numerous facilities and tourist sites to accommodate the arriving guests.

Unfortunately, the charm of the old, rustic, and simple Akara life was rapidly skewed into some uncomfortable directions. The appetites and demands of the off-world visitors were questionable in some cases. They wanted what was available everywhere else in the Federation, both good and bad.

The Akara citizens made individual decisions to comply, or not, rather than follow the old path of consulting the wisdom of the councils of elders. Whether that foretold a future of societal malaise or whether they could retain what made them a great people was yet to be determined.

Progress was happening, but many felt it wasn't a good thing. More than one Akara dinner table was the site of animated discussions about the slide of the morals of some and the adverse influence of too many of the off-world visitors.

Visule and Beca both regretted the development, but neither had any interest in plugging back into the governing process. This was in spite of numerous consultations with local and federal leaders who begged for their return. However, they remained adamant in rejecting further public life.

Brady was pleasantly surprised and said so. "Honey, I've got to say . . ."

However, Beca was riled up by the never-ending issue of pushy visitors who demanded her time.

"Brady, perhaps you should keep your mouth shut, unless you would like to share in feeling my wrath."

He chuckled. "No thanks, I'll pass, I just wanted to—"

"Hush," she snapped, eyeing him grimly.

"I got it," he muttered, smiling sheepishly. His beautiful wife was a wonder, a supremely confident person, and a marvel. She'd grown so much from her broad spectrum of experiences to become a person of great presence, awing anybody who met her. Nowadays, that even included her husband.

Eyeing him balefully, she continued, "Don't you see, sir? I don't want our children enduring this nuisance from the public." She was perturbed, but after a moment she cooled her anger slightly, allowing him to close in and hug her, though in a one-sided embrace. This incarnation of Beca was like a polar opposite of the giddy, starry-eyed version he'd first met in the cave so long ago. Experienced, matured, savvy, and stunning in her beauty, there just weren't enough superlatives to describe her, yet had his missteps caused her to rethink her choice of a mate? He mused sadly, *Is she pondering different directions for her future? Has she found better options? Am I capable of extending trust, or is my nature too much to overcome?*

His great worry about his colossal gaff of conjuring up a problem about Bralic, which could have possibly ruined their marriage, still unnerved him. Whether it was an indelible stain remained to be seen. Seemingly transformed, she was definitely far less forgiving and seemed to have an edge to her that he hadn't seen before. Normally self-assured, Brady began to feel self-doubt and to wonder, was he the best husband for this remarkable woman? Did she still feel the same about him after his errors? She'd spent the bulk of her married life living away, which, combined with his recent missteps, did it add up to disaster? In her view, was he coming up short if she measured him against Bralic? That fear ate at him, despite the fact Bralic had married another.

The ultimate warrior in him had met his ultimate challenge, a wife. That challenge had the name of Beca.

Review Requested:

If you loved this book, would you please provide
a review at Amazon.com?

Lightning Source UK Ltd.
Milton Keynes UK
UKHW04f0708230718
326128UK00002B/185/P